Shimmer

For Kate, Sarah, Naomi and Rachael

Shimmer

Jennifer McBride
and
Lynda Nixon

 FREMANTLE PRESS

And so it begins

'I will not go!' Kora folded her arms and looked away from her father.

'It is not a choice, Kora.' The Emperor placed a hand on her shoulder. 'All genies of royal birth must go.'

She shrugged off his hand. 'I know that, but why now?' Amurru stood quietly by Kora's globe. She strode over to him. 'Tell them, Amurru,' she said, jabbing a finger in the air towards her parents. 'It is madness to send me away now.'

Amurru's yellow eyes blinked slowly. 'To learn how to rule you must first learn how to serve.'

She stomped her foot. This was ridiculous.

Her gaze rested briefly on her younger brother, Atym. They weren't sending him away!

'Please, Mother?'

'You know you have to go sometime,' said her mother.

'It makes sense to go now, to keep you safe while we deal with Vennum.'

'No, it does not make any sense at all. We have been at war with Vennum for eight years.'

'You well know that the situation has changed,' said her mother. 'Vennum's army has grown over the last few months. He has become exceedingly powerful.'

'That is why I should remain here. I am your most powerful genie.'

Her mother's shoulders stiffened. 'I am the Imperial Empress of Genesia, and I have made my decision.'

Kora whirled back to face her father. 'Tell her,' she demanded. 'Tell her that you need me here to help defeat him.'

'It is true that you are the most powerful genie to be born in centuries.' Her father's eyes were gentle. 'But that is why you must go. Vennum wants you more than any other genie. Imagine how it would feel, Kora, if he was to harness you, and force you to destroy Genesia.'

'I do not want to be banished.'

'It will not be forever. Earth duty for you is a requirement under Genesian law. The High Council of Genesia demands it.'

'Please, father. I do not want to go now. You need me.'

'Enough. I will argue with you no more.' The Emperor

signalled to Amurru. 'You will leave immediately, Kora. I command it.'

The air around her began to stir. Her father's command had activated her globe and she was being pulled in against her will. She took one last look around at her home and then glared at her parents.

'I hate you,' she spat. 'I hate you both!'

Arrival

Kora felt the power course through her veins, pumping and tingling until it built to a level far greater than she needed. She gloried in the surge of power, an act of defiance against her father and the rest of the High Council.

'Empress?' Amurru's wheezing voice distracted Kora and the magic exploded from her chest, transforming her glamorous globe so that it would appear to the outside world as just an ordinary rock. The inside, of course, stayed the same — an extravagant mix of Genesia's finest creations designed for an empress, shrunk down along with her by the magic of the globe.

She turned to Amurru, delighted with the disapproval in his eyes.

'Your father would not condone camouflage.' He shuffled towards her, his bad leg dragging on the ground like a forgotten shoelace. 'You must be found.'

The air in her globe still sizzled with the heat of her excessive power. She stared down at him. 'I do not care what you, my father, or the Council think. If I am to be banished to Earth then I shall do as I please.'

Amurru flexed his long, amber wings. 'An empress puts her own interests aside and does what is best for her people.'

'I can do nothing from here,' she spat. 'What is best for my people is for me to be there, fighting with them.'

'No.' He adjusted the wide black belt on his silver suit. 'It was the right decision, for everybody, to send you here.'

'I will find a way to defeat Vennum,' she hissed. 'Even from here.'

'No, Empress. The danger is too great. If Vennum should find you …'

'I am not afraid.'

'Well, you should be, Empress.' Amurru shook his round head. 'You should be!'

She looked away from him in disgust. 'I will not be harnessed.'

Kora stormed around her globe, the loud jingle of her jewellery filling the space, when she felt, rather than saw, Amurru's mood lighten. She slid her eyes in his direction but did not turn her head. His fox-like ears twitched and she knew he had heard something. Armourowls had notoriously exceptional hearing and Amurru's ability had not diminished with age.

The temptation to peek was too strong. Kora lit up the screens that revealed the world outside her globe. A 360-degree panoramic view of this place they called Earth — or more specifically, Panda Rock, Western Australia. Her first look at what was supposed to be her home for who knew how long. Years? Decades?

The view directly in front of her was hot, hard and unwelcoming. Flat grey rocks lay sprawled in the summer sun. They stretched across the land until they reached patches of green scrub. It was hard for her to imagine where the pandas lived.

'This land is barren,' she said, smugly. 'I cannot see any humans.'

'We have landed in a national park for the safety of everybody. But I assure you, Empress, there are many people in the small town nearby.'

'I do not think any human will find me here.'

'We shall see,' murmured Amurru.

His ears twitched and swivelled until they were both straining forwards, his attention completely focused on a tiny patch of shade at the edge of the clearing. The first stirrings of fear snaked through her. A human had emerged and was striding towards them. His heavy footsteps disturbed a lizard basking in the midday sun and she watched in fascination as it darted under a rock to hide.

'All that human will see is a rock.' She forced confidence into her voice. 'He will not be interested in that.'

She held her breath as he neared. Her first sighting of a human boy! She waited for him to simply walk past, but he did not. Was it possible he had seen them land?

Amurru smiled, revealing a row of large, yellowed teeth. 'Curious creatures, humans.'

She watched, horrified, as the human stopped right next to her globe and stared intently down at it from underneath a mop of long, shaggy, dark blond hair. He was not what she had expected. Humans were weaker than genies, they had no power, and she had expected to see that reflected in their build. But this human was tall and strong, with lean muscles that had rippled as he swaggered towards them. She supposed their lack of power meant they needed stronger bodies. His colouring was different to hers as well. Where her skin was a smooth olive brown, his was brown with an underlying fairness — like it was meant to be paler, but life had changed it.

She was jolted out of her musings as her globe was thrust up into the air only to be tossed straight back down again. She immediately used her magic to ensure that they were kept unharmed in the process. She was angry with Amurru, but she would not allow some loathsome human to hurt him.

Her globe was still scorching hot from when she had camouflaged it. She smirked, watching the human dance around shaking his hand. A baboon in a tutu would have more dignity.

'He is hurt.' Amurru's words carried his disapproval.

'Then maybe he should not pick up things that do not belong to him.'

The human squatted down next to her globe. She gasped and stepped back as a pair of piercing blue eyes stared at her. She had never seen eyes like them before in her life. Genies all had brown eyes. They varied from dark to light, but never were they blue, never ever.

For a moment she thought he could see her, but then he looked from his hands to her globe and she realised he was just trying to figure out how a rock had burnt him.

'Curious and persistent,' said Amurru as they watched the human reach out a finger to touch her globe.

The human jerked his finger back as once again her globe seared his skin. Kora sniggered. 'What fool would keep touching something that hurt him?'

The human bent even closer to her globe. This time, he tucked his hand safely beneath his T-shirt and picked it up. Her globe was small and fit easily in the palm of his hand. He was gentler this time and she did not require magic to keep them from being thrown around.

Fear clutched her stomach. She had hoped to have time to figure out a plan to find a way home. To be harnessed so soon would be unbearable.

The human lifted the globe nearer to his face. She could not understand his fascination. Surely to him it was just a rock, a rock like any other rock to be found here on this uninteresting land.

She felt his other hand, also securely beneath his T-shirt, begin to rub her globe and all the air drained from her lungs. She could feel the harnessing begin. With each rub she was being pulled, drawn against her will.

She held on, clawing at the heavy gold bands that had materialised on her wrists and ankles. They tightened and began to glow a deep golden colour, visible evidence that this nightmare was very real.

She reached for Amurru, feeling helpless for the first time in her life. 'Help me,' she pleaded.

She thought she saw compassion in his eyes. 'It is too late,' he answered.

She knew he was right. Pain splintered out from her chest as she resisted the pull of her new master dragging her from her globe.

Amurru's words reached her tormented ears. 'It will be easier if you do not fight it.'

She lifted her chin. She was Kora Archein. Empress. Heir to the Genesian Empire and she would not give in. Who was this human to inflict this on her?

Rub by painful rub her body shattered, not into the usual joyful power rush of shimmering, but into a golden mist of pain, sucking her particle by particle from her temporary home. She tried to focus, to resist the force that was overwhelming her. The boy was a magnet pulling her to him. She could taste his power over her and she hated him for it. With every scrap of power and determination within her she fought him. But it was not enough. She felt herself shimmer. Exhausted, her knees scraped the rocky ground of this place called Earth.

A new master

The boy gaped stupidly at her as she sprang to her feet. Never would she allow herself to grovel on her hands and knees in front of a worthless human!

Kora sucked a deep breath into her aching lungs, and stood as tall as she could, glaring up at him. Her chest still ached from her battle against the pull of the harnessing and the pain made her anger blaze wildly. She lifted her chin higher still, allowing the surge of power that flared in instant response to rumble in her chest, ready to use.

Seconds passed in silence as the boy gathered his wits. Such a slow thinker. But then, hadn't she been told that humans were known to be dimwitted? Her fingers itched to claw at the heavy gold bands that now encircled her wrists and ankles. Repulsive bands that harnessed her to this wretched boy for the rest of his life! But she focused on ignoring them for now, concentrating instead on her new human master standing before her. She had to stay focused if she was to have any hope of tricking him into unharnessing her.

The boy was hunched over, his left hand pressed tightly over his right wrist. He had dropped her globe and it had rolled some distance from his feet. She thought about summoning it to her, but decided to wait. No point letting him know that she was a genie. If humans knew as little as she had been led to believe, then he probably didn't even know genies existed.

So she waited. And waited. Such slow reactions! While she waited she looked him over. He was much bigger than her. Almost impressive. But not with the strange, dull clothing he wore. Probably reflected his personality. Or his intelligence. That thought might have made her laugh if she hadn't been so filled with rage. He wore short, black pants that were loose and baggy. They stopped halfway down his legs, allowing his hairy, knobby knees to poke out from underneath. And his scruffy blue T-shirt was stained, loose and boring, too. It was so … plain. Nothing like the glamorous, glittering clothes worn by Genesian men.

Finally the boy straightened, his hand still tightly gripping his right wrist. It probably hurt like mad. That thought cheered her up somewhat. She knew that the process of harnessing was not only painful for the genie.

Humans experienced an enormous rush of power at the moment of harnessing, usually entering their bodies through the arm that touched the globe, burning and blistering as it went. The burn eventually healed, fading into a long red welt, but they were scarred for life.

The severity of each human's burn varied, depending on the power of the genie being harnessed. A small, bitter smile tugged at one corner of Kora's mouth. Not only was she a very powerful genie, but because she had fought against the harnessing, this human's burn would be nasty in the extreme.

She lost track of how many long, tedious seconds she waited under the blazing heat of the Earth's sun before the human finally thought to close his mouth. He sucked in a long breath that sounded more like a hiss. Then his piercing blue eyes narrowed before they at last dropped away from hers to look down at the harnessing burn on his arm. He carefully lifted the edge of his hand to peek underneath. It was with some satisfaction that she saw the jolt of pain flash across his features when the hot, dry air came into contact with the raw, blistered skin. Why should she be the only one to suffer?

The fresh pain seemed to bring the boy to his senses. He abruptly let go of his arm and reached down to snatch up her globe, not bothering to check if it had cooled off yet. How dare he touch her globe!

The boy turned to face her, the globe clutched in his hand. His mouth lifted in a slight smile. Or perhaps it was a grimace. 'Are you okay?' he asked.

Her anger seethed. Okay? She was stuck on this stupid planet, harnessed to a loathsome human boy, while the worst villain in Genesian history was intent on destroying her family, her people and her homeland. As if she could be okay! She could not answer such a stupid question. She stood glaring at him, inwardly struggling to contain her simmering, rumbling, angry power.

The boy waited for her to speak, and when she did not, asked another question. 'Where did you come from?' But he glanced down at her globe when he spoke, as if he already knew the answer.

'How dare you question me,' she hissed.

She could see she had taken the boy by surprise. He pulled back a little and studied her face for a moment.

She stood in stony silence. He may be her new master, but she was an empress. She did not explain herself to anybody. And he did not know that he was her master. At least, not yet. And if she had her way, not ever.

His eyes drifted to her long, dark hair that hung in a heavy curtain to her waist. Then they moved down to stare at the clothes she wore, made from the exotic Genesian fabrics that she knew would be shimmering like spun gold under the Earth's sun. They took in the gold chains that swung from around her neck, and the jewels that glowed from each of her fingers. They dropped down to her soft, flowing pants, made from the finest silk, and to her bejewelled toes and brown, bare feet that stood planted in the hot, red dust of this wretched place. His eyes never stopped moving, except for once when they came to rest on the huge amber stone that glinted warmly from her exposed bellybutton.

When he finally lifted his eyes back to meet hers, she saw a new knowledge in them. A small twist of fear wound its way up her spine. Perhaps he wasn't as dimwitted as she had supposed.

His eyes widened in astonishment. 'Are you a genie?'

You wish

The stupid boy slapped his hands on his thighs and let out a great whoop of delight. 'I can wish for anything? Anything at all?'

Kora shrugged. 'You cannot wish to harm or change any human.'

She wondered if he was really even listening to her. His eyes were glazed and he was alternating between shaking his head in apparent disbelief and letting out great whooping sounds.

'There's really no limit?' The words tumbled out of his mouth fast. 'I can wish for as much stuff as I want?'

She took a deep, slow breath and nodded. She really hated humans.

'Okay,' he said. 'I wish for … a motorbike. A Honda XR650.'

Her magic stirred and the heavy gold bands that glowed on her wrists and ankles tightened. It was an uncomfortable sensation, as if she wasn't in complete control of her own power. Her magic seemed to flood her body the moment he said 'I wish', but then just flowed directionless until she took control of it. Not that a motorbike required much magic.

She waved her arm and a huge motorbike appeared before them. The relief was instant. The heavy bands remained, but loosened their grip, and she rubbed absently at her wrists.

The boy gaped at the huge bike. 'I can't believe it. You really are a genie!' He stepped forward to run his hand lovingly across the engine. 'It's a four stroke. Air cooled.'

She rolled her eyes. Not only was he human, but he was a human boy.

He swung a leg over the seat and gripped the handlebars. Then turned his head and grinned at her. 'I wish for the keys.'

A quick tightening of her bands and the keys materialised in the ignition. He revved the engine and the bike rocked on the spot like a restless horse at the starting gate. The bike seemed big and heavy, even for a boy his size. Maybe he would fall off and kill himself. She sniggered. That would unharness her.

She thought he might have said something but she could not hear him over the racket the bike was making.

With a look of determination he kicked out the stand and leaned forward over the bike. A twist of his hands and he had roared off in a cloud of dust across the barren land.

Within seconds she felt the tug on her wrists and ankles. He was building up speed and the invisible bond between them tightened painfully. The bands dug deep into her flesh and the next thing she knew, she was being dragged along the hot, hard ground after him, forcing her to use her magic to protect herself.

The boy didn't get very far on his bike before there was an almighty thud and they came to a sliding stop. She looked up to see him lying on the ground clutching the burn on his arm. The bike was on its side, engine still running and sending up angry clouds of dust.

They were still too far apart. Her wrists and ankles were torturously painful. The boy was looking at her. He staggered to his feet and lumbered toward her. The relief was bliss.

He slumped down on the dirt next to her. He carefully lifted his hand from the blistering welt on his arm as if he wanted to be sure the pain wasn't about to come to life again.

'So what on earth was that?'

'Whilst I am your genie we cannot be more than a hundred metres apart.'

'You mean you have to be hanging around all the time?' His expression was horrified. 'What if I want some privacy?'

'Then you can wish to unharness me.'

'Unharness you?' His eyes narrowed suspiciously. 'Like, set you free?'

A small flicker of hope fluttered in her belly at the word 'free'. 'That is correct.' She could see his slow mind working.

'But then you wouldn't be my genie any more?'

'It is for you to decide,' she said, looking pointedly at his arm. 'How much do you value your privacy?'

He frowned. 'But if I unharness you, does that mean I won't get any more wishes?'

Freedom was so close she could taste it. 'Wish for all you want now,' she tempted him. 'As many wishes as you like.' How much could a human want, anyway? 'And then you could unharness me and be on your way. Alone!'

She waited. She could see the idea appealed to him as his stupid human mind sifted through all the pathetic things that he could wish for. But then he shook his head. 'No. I think I'll see how having a genie goes for a while.'

Anger and disappointment coursed through her. 'Then you had better get used to having me around.' She arched her eyebrows at him. 'All the time!'

She saw a flash of doubt cross his face and he rubbed his chin. 'So, you will stay my genie until I wish for you not to be?'

'Or until you die.' She smiled sweetly and glanced at the bike. 'Whichever happens to come first.'

He jerked his head in the direction of the bike. 'Can you do something about that noise?'

With a brief wave of her wrist the bike disappeared. The sudden silence was unsettling. She felt his eyes on her in silent contemplation. Would the thought of having her around all the time be enough to make him unharness her after just a few wishes? Could she make life so awful for him that he would hate having her around? How she yearned for her freedom.

'So how does it work?' His words broke into her thoughts. 'Do you come and live at my house?'

She sighed. Of course no human was going to give up a genie easily.

'I will live in my own home.' She met his blank look. 'The one you stole.'

'Of course,' he said, touching the pocket that held her globe. 'You live in the rock that fell out of the sky.'

Using magic, Kora lifted her globe out of his pocket. It travelled through the air to land safely in the palm of her hand.

'Not a rock.' She waved her free hand across it and the camouflage dropped away, revealing the most exquisitely beautiful golden vessel. 'A globe.'

'That's amazing.' He looked up. 'But I thought genies lived in oil lamps? Or bottles?'

Kora waved her hand again, and the beautiful globe turned into an old-fashioned oil lamp, its ancient silver battered and tarnished. 'Our globes can appear however we want them to.'

He shook his head in amazement.

'So do I just call out "genie" when I want you?'

'My name is Kora.' The thought of him summoning her for every stupid whim irritated her and she used her most condescending voice. 'But you may call me Empress.'

'Well, Empress,' he sniggered, imitating her tone of voice. 'My name is David. But you may call me Master.'

She stiffened at the word 'master'. Getting to her feet she looked down her regal nose at him. 'Some advice, Master,' she said. 'Be very, very, careful what you wish for.'

She allowed her words to hang ominously in the air between them, and then, in a perfect golden mist, slowly shimmered into the haven of her globe.

All that glitters

Kora sank gratefully into her favourite seat and curled her toes into the luxurious carpet. Glittering threads of silver and gold were woven through the silk fabrics that lined the walls and covered the cushions in her globe. They sparkled in the soft light that glowed from the hundreds of tiny coloured lamps that floated in the air above her.

She sipped at the icy fruit drink that appeared in her hand. 'This Earth climate is dreadful,' she told Amurru. 'Humans do not seem to have any control over the weather!'

'Mmm,' replied Amurru absently. He sat in the small seat that had been specially designed to support his winged back, his eyes on the human boy.

Kora looked back out at the boy. She liked the place that David had chosen for her globe. It was perched on a small shelf on the opposite side of the room from his bed, sandwiched between a silver football trophy and a photograph showing a much younger David beside an older man in an army uniform.

From this vantage point she could look down on the boy, and she could keep an eye on what he was doing almost anywhere in the room. At the moment he was stretched out on his bed surrounded by new gadgets. His face was all concentration as he jabbed away at a games console.

'He is lazy and boring,' said Kora. 'All he wants are stupid toys.' Lying next to David on his bed was a pile of new games for the console, and an iPod, its unused earphones dangling down onto the floor. Balanced precariously on his chest was an iPhone that flashed and jiggled with stupid messages from his friends that made him smirk. On the beige carpet by his bed sat a new laptop computer, still in its box, and on the far wall, amongst a tangle of posters of motorbikes and rock bands, hung an enormous, new TV. 'And he is greedy.'

Amurru nodded. 'It is true that he has much to learn.' His yellow eyes were shrewd. 'But it is early days, Empress.'

Kora screwed her face up. Her iced drink vanished and was replaced by a glass bowl piled high with wild red berries. 'He is a human, Amurru. I doubt he can learn anything.' She popped one of the berries into her mouth.

'Perhaps you are right, Empress.' Amurru sighed, the air rattling out of his lungs in a gust of wheezy breath. 'But he may surprise you, yet.'

She doubted that anything the boy could do would surprise her. Hadn't he already proven he was every bit as dumb as the humans in all the old stories? All those stupid wishes he had made since they had arrived at his house! She looked back at him. He must have grown bored with the game he'd been playing. He had dropped it onto the bed beside him and was now lying back against his pillows with his hands behind his head listening to his iPod. And he was looking straight at her.

She stared back at him, glad that he couldn't see her. The panoramic viewing screens inside her globe were one-way vision only. All he would be able to see would be the same dusty, grey rock he had first picked up.

The corners of her mouth lifted as she looked at the white bandage he had clumsily wrapped around the burn on his right arm. He had wished for her to heal it, or at least to stop it from hurting so much. She really had enjoyed telling him that that was one wish she couldn't grant. Genie magic was the most powerful magic in the universe. But there were some exceptions to its use and one of those exceptions was humans. Humans were impervious to genie magic. No human could ever be harmed, killed or changed in any way by a genie. There were two exceptions to this — the ancient process of harnessing and the ability to be shimmered from place to place by a genie.

'The boy is thinking about something,' said Amurru, interrupting her thoughts.

'I am sure that is a very difficult task for him,' she sneered.

Amurru laughed, coughing out a strange choking sound. 'Nevertheless, he has something on his mind, Empress.'

'He is probably trying to think of a new toy he has not wished for yet.' Kora's face was scornful, but she shifted uncomfortably in her seat. She didn't like to admit that David's direct blue gaze unsettled her, even knowing that he couldn't see her. 'Or maybe he is just thinking about his stomach.' She looked at the crushed bundle of empty fast-food wrappers that had been squashed into the little rubbish bin next to his bed.

'It is more than that, I think, Empress.' He nodded his head thoughtfully. 'He is troubled.'

'I doubt that, Amurru,' scoffed Kora. 'What troubles could he possibly have?' She waved away the glass bowl and curled her feet up on the cushion beside her. 'The only things he thinks about are toys, food and avoiding his chores.'

'Mmm, perhaps,' murmured Amurru. His voice sounded distracted and Kora glanced at him. She saw his ears twitch, then swivel around towards the bedroom door.

'Someone is here, Empress.'

Kora sat up straighter in her seat and looked towards the door. Within seconds she heard the click-click-click of high-heeled shoes as they tapped down the passage towards David's bedroom. She glanced at David. He was deep in thought and, with the earphones in, he hadn't heard the footsteps yet.

'David?' called out a soft, gentle voice.

At the sound of his name he lurched off the bed in surprise, his face panicky and unsure. He took one tentative step towards the door and Kora thought he was going to rush out of the room to greet his visitor, but she arrived in the doorway before he could move.

'There you are, David,' she said in a singsong voice. A short woman wearing shiny, pink high heels and black trousers appeared in the bedroom doorway. She was a little on the plump side, Kora thought, and plain looking. But there was something sweet about her. Her eyes were blue, like David's, only hers were much softer. Her long, fair hair was pulled back from her face into a ponytail, giving her a youthful, sporty look, and she wore a navy shirt with the words 'Panda Rock DVD & Games Hire' written across the front pocket. One hand clutched a bundle of unopened mail.

Tiny creases fanned out from around her eyes, and she wore virtually no make-up apart from a smudge of pink lipstick.

'Mum!' exclaimed David. Kora thought she detected a note of panic in his voice. 'You're home from work early.'

'David, the house is lovely,' cooed the woman. Her eyes sparkled. 'It's spotless! You must have cleaned all day.'

'Oh,' he mumbled, sidling further away from his bed. 'Yeah, I cleaned up for you.'

'And you've done all your chores as well,' continued his mother. 'And the front garden has been weeded!' She shook her head in amazement. 'You even swept up the driveway. How on earth did you get time for all that?'

'Um, well,' he mumbled, 'I thought it would be nice for you.' He moved towards his mother, his face turning a strange shade of red. 'Come on, Mum,' he said, 'I'll make you a cup of tea.'

He took his mother's arm and tried to turn her from the room, but it was too late. The smile on his mother's face froze as her eyes caught sight of her son's bed. She sucked in her breath as she took in the mountain of new electronic equipment. Her gaze dropped down to the laptop on the floor before moving up to the electronics piled on his desk. And then she lifted her eyes to the far wall. A look of horror and disbelief spread across her face. She began to pant in short, anxious gasps and her eyes filled with tears as they locked onto David's forty-inch-high definition plasma TV.

Can you keep a secret?

Amurru's ears twitched madly.

Kora frowned. 'What's the matter with you?'

'I have been summoned.'

'My father?'

Amurru nodded. He glanced out towards David. 'It seems we are both being summoned.'

She ignored the uncomfortable sensation of having her name called by her new master. 'He can wait. I want to see what my father wants.'

Amurru turned one ear to David. 'He is impatient.'

Her bangles jingled. 'So am I. Now go.'

Amurru shrugged and closed his eyes. The wrinkles on his face seemed to flatten out a little and his normally short, wheezy breath deepened. He rolled his shoulders and his long, shiny amber wings extended, stretching downwards until they brushed against the floor. Then they curled and wrapped tightly around him, forming a translucent armoured cocoon. She could always feel the moment he projected. It was like a great source of energy had vanished. It was a skill peculiar to armourowls, the ability to leave their body behind and project themselves in energy form to another place, where they would appear like a small moving image of themselves, a hologram, able to talk and listen to whoever was there. It was exhausting for them and also incredibly dangerous. The body left behind was vulnerable, protected only by its shield of wings.

She paced the floor. Something was wrong. It was too soon for her father to make contact. The calling of her name increased in both frequency and demand and she glared out at the stupid human.

'Kora!'

His tone shifted to one of command and the force of it caused her to shimmer from her globe.

'What do you want now?'

He looked at her accusingly. 'I've been calling you.'

'So?'

'Didn't you see my mum?' His arm flailed in the air. 'She's gonna think I stole all this stuff.'

She stared at him in disbelief. Amurru was in her globe projecting himself back to Genesia and David had summoned her away because of a problem with his mum.

He really was completely unaware of anybody but himself.

She wrinkled her nose at the assault of Earth smell that invaded her senses. 'Do you want me to get rid of your new toys?'

'Of course not.' He glanced lovingly up at his new plasma. 'I want you to come and meet my mum. Explain things.'

'You idiotic human.' She lifted herself up to her full height. Her power rumbled in her chest and the air sizzled like an approaching thunderstorm. 'You must tell no one about me. Do you understand?'

David stood a little taller. 'You never said it was a secret.'

'Every human in history that has harnessed a genie and not kept the secret has been murdered.'

David's head snapped up. 'Why?'

'So they can harness the genie for themselves. Humans are very bad at keeping secrets. Tell one person and it will not be long until your secret is out. And then it will not just be your life that will be endangered.'

She was pleased to see the look of shock on David's face until she realised it was not her words that had caused it. He was staring intently at her globe. She turned in time to see that Amurru had left the globe and was shuffling towards David.

David's jaw fell open. 'What on earth is that?'

Before she could answer Amurru extended a short, fuzzy hand up towards David in traditional Earth custom. 'Hello, David. My name is Amurru.'

David looked gigantic towering over Amurru. The tips of his ears barely reached David's waist.

David bent his knees and reached down. He tentatively clasped Amurru's short, stumpy fingers with their yellowed, pointy claws. 'Um … hi.'

Kora felt like she was going to explode. 'What are you doing out here?'

'I am most pleased to finally meet with you, David.' Amurru removed his hand from David's grip and turned to Kora. 'I have news, Empress.' Amurru glanced at David. 'And it affects both of you.'

Her earlier unease returned with full force. She knew something was wrong. 'My father?'

'Everyone at home is fine.' Amurru assured her but his voice was grave. 'But they believe Vennum is monitoring Earth.'

'He knows I am here?'

'We cannot be sure.'

'How could he know so soon?'

'There was a power spike.'

She did not need to ask when. Amurru did not say

it but she felt the accusation. The excessive power she had used in disguising her globe and fighting against being harnessed would have registered as a power spike to anyone looking out for it.

'As long as you are careful he will not find you.' Amurru's yellow eyes lifted to David. 'Both of you will need to be careful.'

'Careful of what? And what's a vennum?'

'I told you it was a waste of time sending me here.' Kora folded her arms. 'I told you all.'

Amurru ignored her. 'Vennum is the most dangerous threat Genesia has ever faced.'

Kora knew the dimwit would need further explanation. 'Genesia is where we come from. And Vennum is half-human and half-genie — he has the long life of a genie but no magic of his own. This makes him very dangerous. His human side enables him to harness genie after genie and his long life means that most of them will remain harnessed to him for the rest of their lives. He is only twenty-two years old, and yet he already has dozens of genies under his control.'

'So I could have more than one genie?'

Unbelievable! Could he be more selfish? She looked pointedly at the bandaged burn on his arm. 'Can you imagine what that would feel like?'

She liked the shudder she saw pass through him.

'Why would he need so many genies? Can't one grant all his wishes?' asked David.

Amurru coughed and wheezed. 'His wish is to destroy the Empire. He will crush the royal blood line and rule Genesia himself.'

She could see David's mind at work. It may be slow but she felt sure he was indeed piecing it together. 'It's you he wants.' He poked an accusing finger at her. 'Royal blood. You're hiding here and you need me to keep your secret.'

She flung her dark hair back off her face. 'And if Vennum does find me, who is it that he will need to kill to harness me?'

'I'll wish you unharnessed.'

She sniggered. 'I doubt Vennum would be inclined to wait while you did that.'

Amurru shuffled between them. 'There is no reason for Vennum to find you.' His wrinkled round face fixed on David. 'You must keep the secret to protect both you and your family.' Amurru then turned to her. 'And you, Empress, need to control your temper.'

'If this Vennum is monitoring Earth, then what exactly is he looking for?'

She sighed. 'Large power spikes.'

Amurru nodded seriously. 'For example, any wish that controls the elements would put you both in danger.'

David frowned. 'But other wishes are okay?'

'Your stupid human wishes require very little magic.' She noticed Amurru's wheezing had worsened. He would be tired from projecting. 'And you should rest.'

They all turned at the sound of a car door closing. 'Rodney's here.' David sighed. 'Mum said I had to explain to both of them where I got all this stuff from.'

'Then make a choice, human. Unharness me or keep me a secret!'

He stared thoughtfully at her. 'I'll keep your secret, Empress. But I'll tell you this. Having a genie isn't all it's cracked up to be.'

His mother's voice carried down the hall. 'David. You've got some explaining to do!'

Mum's the word

Amurru's ears twitched. 'The boy seeks you, Empress.'

Kora nodded. She would not wait around for the stupid human boy to haul her from her globe again like a common genie. She hated having to obey his commands. She threw a quick grin at Amurru and shimmered out of her globe into David's room. Humans were so slow, even when they were hurrying, and she knew she had plenty of time before he arrived in his room. Two or three seconds, at least.

One small flick of her hand saw all his new stuff fly from his bed to pile up on the old wooden desk. His pillows arranged themselves at the head of his bed, and she quickly reclined back on them, looking as relaxed as she could on such a lumpy, old mattress. Ugh, how could anyone actually sleep on such an uncomfortable thing?

David burst into the room, closing the door behind him. 'Kora?' he whispered. 'Come out. Now!' He started towards her globe before spotting her lounging on his bed. His eyes narrowed at her but he made no comment.

'Yes, master?' she replied, sweetly. 'Is there something you want?'

He stared down at her on his bed. One hand shoved at the heavy, long fringe that fell forward across his eyes. 'Quick, Kora,' he said. 'Make me a certificate.'

'A certificate?' She lifted one eyebrow. 'I do not know what you mean.'

'Kora, there isn't much time!' His breath huffed out impatiently. 'Just do it.'

She pushed herself into a sitting position. 'Your bed is not very comfortable, master.'

'Then get off it,' hissed David, 'and make me that certificate. Mum's waiting.'

A flash of anger coursed through her and her power rumbled unsteadily in response. In her entire life no one had ever spoken to her in such a way. 'Why should I?'

David's eyes darted nervously to the closed bedroom door. 'Because I wish it.'

She felt the bands around her wrists begin to tighten when he spoke the words 'I wish'. A soft, golden glow radiated from them and her power stirred restlessly, ready and waiting.

He moved closer to her, keeping his voice low. 'On

the first line write, "Congratulations to David Wolfe".'
His brow creased in concentration. 'Then on a line below
that write, "Winner of the Volunteer Bush Fire Brigade's
Annual Giant Christmas Raffle".' He stood up and paced
anxiously across the room to listen briefly at the door. 'And
put a signature at the bottom. And today's date.' He strode
back to face her. 'And put it in a black frame.'

Kora's mouth twisted in distaste, but she lifted her
hand and the framed certificate appeared in it. She handed
it to him with a glare. 'Surely your parents did not fall for
such a stupid story?' Her voice rang with contempt.

'The local Bush Fire Brigade holds a giant Christmas
raffle every year.' His gaze lifted to meet hers. 'And by the
way, they are not my parents.'

'Really?' She was surprised. 'Not your parents?'

'No.' He shook his head emphatically. 'Marcia's my
mum.' He glanced at the photograph on the shelf next to
her globe. 'But Rodney's not my father. He's my mother's
new boyfriend.'

Kora's eyes drifted to the framed photograph on the
shelf. Her eyes looked over the tall man standing with his
arm around a much younger David. 'He looks like you,'
she said. Two pairs of piercing blue eyes gazed back at
her. The older man's were perhaps a slightly darker blue
than David's, with laugh lines fanning outwards from the

corners, but otherwise they were the same. But it wasn't just the eyes. She could see other similarities, now that she knew. There was the same dark blond hair, although cut much shorter, and the same cocky grin. She pursed her lips. They were both good-looking, really. For humans.

David sighed. 'I think I've grown a bit taller than he was.'

Her eyes flew back to his face. 'Than he was? Is your father dead?'

'No!' His face darkened as he met Kora's gaze. 'I'll never believe that!'

She wanted to ask more, but a sharp intake of breath had both their heads spinning towards the bedroom door.

His mother stood in the doorway, an astonished look on her face. 'David?' His mother's eyes roved over Kora, widening as they took in her golden, silk harem pants, the glittering jewels and her bare feet. 'I thought I heard voices in here. I didn't know you had a guest.'

Kora looked at David. He stood frozen to the spot, his mouth gaping open and the framed certificate clutched in his hands. She shook her head in disgust. It seemed that humans spent a lot of time with their mouths wide.

His mother reached over and took the certificate without looking at it. Instead, she looked at Kora. 'What beautiful eyes,' she said, smiling. She held her hand out.

'Hello, dear,' she said. 'I don't think we've met before. I'm Marcia Wolfe, David's mother.'

She reached out and took his mother's hand. 'I am Kora.' She threw a smug look at David. He stared at her, saying nothing, but his eyes were narrowed in silent warning.

'What a glamorous costume you're wearing.' Marcia looked her up and down. 'Are you on your way to a fancy dress party, then?'

'Yes, that's right.' David jumped into the conversation, speaking a little too quickly. 'There's a fancy dress party tonight.'

Marcia regarded him suspiciously. 'And were you planning on going too, David?' Her brow furrowed. 'Is that why you did so much cleaning up around the house today? So we'd be more likely to let you go?'

'No, no,' he stammered. 'Anyway, I can't go. I, um, don't even have a costume.'

Kora smirked at him. 'That will not be a problem,' she said sweetly. 'I have brought a costume for you to wear.' She pointed towards the corner of the room, behind his mother, where a brown paper parcel appeared on the floor.

Marcia smiled. 'Good,' she said. 'Then we'd better have an early dinner.' She smiled at Kora. 'You'll join us, of course, dear.'

David's mouth opened to object, but his mother cut in smoothly. 'I'm sure Rodney would love to meet your new friend.' She raised one eyebrow. 'And besides, I can't wait to see your costume.'

Hmm ... yum. Tofu!

Kora followed David down the narrow passageway. The horrid Earth scent intensified and she realised they had reached the kitchen. A middle-aged man was standing by the kitchen stove. He scuffed over to Kora and reached out his hand. 'I'm Rodney.'

She placed her hand in his sweaty grasp. 'Kora.'

Rodney's fair skin reddened. 'Glad that you're joining us for dinner, Kora.' He flicked David with the tea towel. 'So what's with the soldier outfit?'

'Fancy dress.'

Rodney scratched a big patch of angry red eczema on his arm. 'It suits you.'

Kora smiled to herself, thinking about the costume she had intended for David. A fat, hairy baboon suit, complete with a tiny, sparkly pink tutu — that was the costume that really suited him. Of course David hadn't thought it was funny at all and had immediately wished for a new one.

'Take a seat, kids.' Rodney turned back to the stove. 'Dinner's nearly ready.'

Kora pulled out her chair at the table. It was heavy. Curled up on it was an enormously fat ginger cat. It opened one eye at her and then leapt to its feet. Arching its back it let out an almighty hiss.

'Cuddles!'

At David's voice the cat twitched its ears and leapt from the chair. Skulking from the room it turned to hiss one last time at her before it disappeared.

David smirked. 'You seem to have a way with animals.'

He was such an idiot. Even for a human. She ignored him and sank gracefully into the chair. She could hear the click, click, click of Marcia's high-heeled shoes and a moment later she burst into the kitchen.

'Hmm, that smells great.'

Kora wrinkled her nose. Surely Marcia was joking, it smelt disgusting.

'So, where's the party tonight?'

David shifted restlessly in his chair. 'Umm … at Tiffany's house.'

'She invited you?' His mother's head whipped around. 'Even after she dumped you?'

David shrugged but his face reddened. 'Yeah.'

Kora tried to hide her snigger. It seemed even the

human girls could not stand him.

She could feel Marcia's eyes on her. 'Who else is going?'

'I dunno, Mum.' David pushed a hand through his shaggy hair. 'Just Hammer and the usual crowd I guess.'

Marcia nodded thoughtfully. 'Be home by midnight. And for goodness sake would you cut that hair!'

'Dinner's up,' said Rodney. He placed a steaming bowl of pasta in front of each of them. 'Hope you like tofu and mung beans.'

David groaned. 'This isn't that gluten-free pasta again, is it?'

Rodney smiled at Kora and patted his stomach. 'I'm gluten-intolerant. I hope you don't mind.'

Kora smiled. 'Of course not.' She placed her fork into the pasta and wound the long hideous strands around it.

'See, Kora likes it.' Marcia said to David. 'It's good for all of us to make healthier choices.'

'That's right, David.' Kora turned her head so that only David could see her transform the sticky tofu pasta into a decadent chocolate cake. 'Healthy and delicious.'

He glared back at her and she smiled. She thought for a moment he was going to whisper a wish but Rodney interrupted him. 'What happened to your arm?'

'Burnt it on the kettle.' David pushed at his food with his fork. 'It's all right.'

It was strange sitting there listening to Marcia and Rodney grill David. Although she liked watching him squirm there was also something familiar about it and a wave of homesickness washed over her. She wondered what her mum and dad were doing now. Were they thinking about her? And what about Atym? She had never imagined she would miss her annoying brother so much.

'Are you all right, dear?'

She looked up and realised Marcia had been talking to her. She wanted to say no, I am not all right. I want to go home and I miss my family. In fact, right now she missed them so badly she would settle for her globe and Amurru.

She put her fork down, no longer interested in eating. 'Sorry, I was daydreaming.'

'I was just saying what an unusual accent you have. Have you moved here recently?'

David cut in before she could answer.

'She's here as an exchange student.' He pushed his plate away. 'We should get going, the party starts in half an hour.'

Rodney's face dropped. 'But you haven't finished.'

'I'm not really hungry.'

'I saw the empty wrappers in your room this afternoon.' Marcia looked accusingly at her son. 'No wonder you're not hungry.'

'Yeah, sorry, Mum.'

'Oh, go on then.' Marcia waved her arms. 'But don't be late.'

David stood up, tall and straight in his army costume. He looked eager to get out of the house. Kora slid her chair back and rose to stand beside him. She couldn't wait to leave either.

Stargazing

It was a beautiful summer's evening. The moon hadn't risen yet and the sky was filled with a million gleaming stars. The scorching heat of the day had finally blown away with the arrival of a soft, balmy breeze that had travelled in from the Indian Ocean, which David had told her was quite some distance away, beyond the city. Even the disgusting Earth smell she so detested seemed softer and more fragrant.

Darkness had settled quickly over the forest once the sun had dropped down beyond the horizon. But even without the moon she could still see quite well by the faint glow of light that reflected up from the small township of Panda Rock, four or five kilometres behind them on the other side of David's house.

David sighed loudly as he stretched out beside her. 'This lounge is really comfortable,' he said, sinking down into the plump, silk cushions she had provided for them.

'It's more comfortable than my bed!'

'Anything would be more comfortable than your bed.' Kora was stretched out on a matching lounge beside him. They were on the very top of a hill, or at least, the top of a very large mound of rocks, not far from where she had been harnessed that morning.

She let out a long, tired breath and dropped her head back to rest against the cushions. It seemed impossible that it was still only her first day on Earth. So much had happened since she had arrived. Somehow it seemed like an eternity since she had last seen her parents, and had spoken those hurtful, parting words to them.

They both lay quietly for some time, lost in their thoughts. Kora stared out across the treetops towards the glittering city lights visible on the horizon. After the stress of the day, the night was so peaceful. Or at least it was until the silence was broken by the sound of David's mobile phone beeping. A small circle of light lit up around him as he read the new text message, then he glanced up at her, a mischievous grin on his face. 'Do you like camping, Kora?'

'I have never been camping,' she replied. 'I do not know if I would like it. Anyway, what does it matter? I have no intention of taking up this pastime. I have far more important things to concern myself with.' She lifted her chin, but her eyes sidled over to him warily. 'Why do you ask me this?'

'Well, it looks like you're going to get to try it pretty soon.' David pressed a few buttons on his phone and slipped it back into his pocket. 'Every year a few of us go camping in the summer holidays, and it's Hammer's turn to organise it this year.' He waved his hand down towards the bottom of the hill. 'We usually set up camp down there on the other side of the rock, near where the creek comes out.' He raised his eyebrows at her. 'I guess you'll have to come, too, this year. Now that you can't be more than a hundred metres away from me.'

Kora flopped back against the lounge. Great! A camping trip with David's friends was the last thing she needed. David relaxed back against his cushions. Kora blew out a long, calming breath. It seemed she was going to be stuck with David and his life on Earth for the time being. For now she might as well just try to enjoy the peace of the night.

She closed her eyes and tilted her face into the wind, letting the soft breeze lift the hair from her face. She tried to focus on the silence, but she soon realised the night was far from quiet. All around them were the sounds of unseen life. Kora listened to the rustling, scratching and screeching noises coming from the forest and wondered what strange creatures of the dark were out there making such a racket. Maybe camping out would be scarier than she thought?

She glanced across at David. 'Do you think we might see some pandas tonight?'

He laughed. 'There aren't any pandas in Australia, Kora.'

'But this place is called Panda Rock!'

'That's because from a distance the mound of rocks we're lying on looks like a panda sitting up on its hind legs.' He turned his head to the side to look at her. 'You can even see the outline of its face. And there's a darker patch of rock near the top that gives it a black patch over its eye.' He shrugged. 'People drive up here from the city to see it.' He turned and pointed back towards the small township. 'They even named the town of Panda Rock after it.'

Kora's smile faded. 'So there are no pandas here at all?' She couldn't hide the disappointment in her voice, but David didn't seem to notice.

'Nope. Never have been and never will be,' he declared.

She shook her head in disbelief. 'That is the only reason I had for choosing to come to Panda Rock,' she said. 'I have always wanted to see a panda.'

'Can't you just use your magic to see one?'

'I suppose I could bring one here,' she agreed, 'but that would be cruel and upsetting for the poor panda. And it might not survive the shock.'

'Couldn't you go and visit one?'

'Not really.' She shook her head. 'There are no pandas on Genesia, and I was harnessed by you as soon as I arrived on Earth.' She screwed her face up at him. 'I cannot ever be more than a hundred metres from you, remember?'

'Yeah, sorry about that,' he said, not sounding the least bit sorry. 'Guess you'll just have to miss out, then.'

'Oh, it does not matter.' She sighed, slumping back against the cushions. 'It is to be expected, I suppose. I had thought that if I had to come to Earth, I might at least get to see something nice.'

'Do you really hate being here so much?'

She shrugged. 'It is more that I hate not being able to be at home.' She turned her head, her troubled eyes meeting his blue gaze.

'Where exactly is your home?'

She dragged her eyes away from his, turning her head so she could stare up at the stars. Thinking about her home and the family she had left behind made her heart ache.

'It is hard to describe exactly where Genesia is. It is in this universe, but is well hidden from humans. You might say it is another dimension.'

'Is it far away?'

'Not so far away,' she said. 'It is a complete solar system, just like yours. It has planets, moons, stars, a beautiful sun … everything.' Kora's voice was wistful as she thought about her home.

'It's hard to believe there's another whole dimension out there that we know nothing about,' said David. 'Is it identical to ours, then?'

'No,' replied Kora. 'There is one lovely, golden sun, just like yours. And although the constellations are different, there is a whole galaxy of stars sparkling in the sky.' She waved her hand across the glittering view above them. 'But we have only four planets in our solar system, and each planet has four moons. The moons are all different sizes, and some of them are red or blue instead of yellow.' She grinned at him. 'They all rise at different times during the night, and they crisscross each other like fireworks in slow motion as they travel across the sky in different directions.'

'Wow!' David blew out his breath. 'That sounds incredible, Kora.' He sat up on the lounge and rested his elbows on his knees. 'So Genesia is one of the four planets, then?'

She nodded. 'Yes, it is the third planet from the sun, just like yours.'

'So it's similar to the Earth?'

'No.' She shook her head. 'It is nothing at all like your Earth. Genesia is the most beautiful place in all existence. The city is filled with glittering, golden buildings and the weather is always perfect.'

David screwed his nose up. 'That sounds pretty boring, actually,' he said. 'I love the wild storms we get here. And the changing seasons.'

'The forests there are very beautiful, too,' she said. 'Green and lush and filled with the most amazing creatures.' She glanced across at him. 'Of course, the seasons do change in the forests. It is only inside the city, within the Genesian Protection Zone, that we control the weather.'

'So is Genesia the name of the planet or the name of the city?' asked David.

'It is both,' replied Kora. 'Genesia, the planet, has only one continent with one capital city, and both are simply known as Genesia.'

'Perhaps you could take me there?' he asked. 'I'd like to see it.'

She shook her head. 'That will never happen. It is strictly forbidden for any human to enter Genesia.'

'Why?'

'Think about it, David. What do you think would happen if a human entered a city full of genies?'

'Oh, yes, I see.' He looked down at the bandaged burn on his arm. 'Every genie he came across would be harnessed.'

'Yes. Genies are powerful, but we do have one weakness. We can be harnessed.' She threw a meaningful look at him. 'Not only could that one human end up controlling all of Genesia, but the combined power of all the harnessed genies would be enough to destroy the entire universe.'

David gave a low whistle. 'But surely only a madman would want to destroy the universe? After all, he has to live in it himself.'

'Perhaps,' she agreed. 'But if a human harnessed many genies, the massive amount of power would be too much for their human brain. It would send the person insane, so he would indeed be a madman.'

'What would happen if I wished to go to Genesia?'

'It would be the same as if you wished to harm another human. Nothing would happen.'

David frowned. 'Then how did Vennum get there?'

'A genie has the power to take a human there, but it is forbidden to do so. Vennum has rogue genies in his army that are prepared to do it.'

'So that means you can't go home?'

'Not until you either die or wish to unharness me,' she replied. 'And even then, only if I can get away before being harnessed by another human.'

'Exactly how long do genies usually live?' he asked. 'You might die before me.'

'Unlikely.' She smiled at that idea. 'Genies live at least ten times longer than humans. Unless they are killed somehow, most genies live to celebrate their one thousandth birthday.' She shrugged. 'So being harnessed to a human only takes up a small part of our life.'

His eyes widened. 'Really? You will live to be a thousand?' He shook his head in disbelief. 'So when we're both eighty, will you look the same age as me?'

'No, thank goodness,' she replied. 'At first Genesian children do age at around the same rate as humans. But that stops when we are fully grown.' She frowned, thinking. 'I guess that would be at about the age of sixteen.'

'And then?'

'We still age but very, very slowly. It takes a thousand years for us to age as much as you would in a hundred years.'

David stared at her. He was obviously having trouble getting his head around everything she had told him.

'It is a shame you will never see Genesia, David.' A small smile lit her face as she thought of her home. 'It is a very beautiful place. No one is poor or hungry, and there is virtually no illness. It is a wonderful place to live.' She shrugged. 'At least, it was. Until Vennum showed up.'

She sat up on her lounge. She couldn't bear another moment of talking about that vile half-human monster and what he could be doing to her family and her people at that very moment. She looked at David. 'It must be getting late,' she said. 'Perhaps we should return home?' She longed to curl up inside the haven of her globe.

David glanced at the old gold watch he wore on his wrist. Kora had noticed the watch earlier. He had been wearing it all day. The brown leather strap was battered and creased, and the plain, round face was scratched. But the main reason she had noticed it was because it didn't work. The watch had stopped at 3.17.

'We can't go home yet,' he said. 'It's not late enough. We need to stay out until at least midnight.' He shrugged sheepishly. 'Mum would never believe that the party finished earlier than that.'

Kora yawned. 'In that case,' she said, 'it is your turn to talk.'

'What do you want to know?'

She shrugged. 'Tell me about your father.'

Dreaming

Kora sat bolt upright in bed. What was that dreadful screeching? The terrible noise was getting closer. She finally realised it was coming from a human and the accompanying click, click, click of high heels told her it was David's mother. Stupid humans.

She rose from her bed and moved to look out of her globe into David's room.

Amurru joined her. 'Sleep well, Empress?'

Kora knew Amurru had been a supporter of sending her to Earth. She spoke without even looking at him. 'No. I dreamt of home.'

'Maybe you will enjoy your second day on Earth better, Empress.'

She could taste the contempt on her tongue. 'Two days on Earth is two days too many.'

The morning light streamed through the open window of David's room and she could see him in his bed. How could he still be asleep through that racket? The door to his room burst open.

'David Wolfe,' shouted his mother. 'You'd better have a good explanation for this!'

David sat up and rubbed his eyes. 'What is it?'

'Four Fs,' she said waving a bit of paper wildly in the air. 'You told me you were doing better at school.'

'Could have been worse,' he shrugged. 'I could have failed five subjects.'

'Don't you take that attitude with me, young man.' Red angry blotches broke out on Marcia's face. 'You're lucky I didn't open your report until this morning or there is no way you would have been gallivanting about with your new girlfriend last night.'

Kora hissed. 'As if I could ever be interested in a human.'

His mother stomped further into the room to hover over David. 'You are grounded. For the entire school holidays.'

'Come on, Mum. That's not fair.'

'Your attitude is what's not fair. You can spend the holidays at home doing chores and thinking about this report and how you could have done better. You can start today by fixing the fence, chopping the wood and cleaning out the chook yard.'

'What about my job?'

'You can go to work on Saturdays, but that's all.'

'And the camping trip?'

'You can forget that, too. You're grounded!'

'That sucks.' David pushed his hand through his shaggy hair.

Marcia leaned over until she was eye level with David. 'Not as much as this report sucks.' She grabbed a big handful of his hair. 'And get your hair cut after work on Saturday or I'll cut it off myself.'

With a yank of his hair she stormed out of the room, slamming the door on her way out.

Kora smiled. 'I thought father had a temper.'

'Can you not see he is suffering, Empress?'

'Oh, poor baby with his little human problems. What about me!'

'The universe is bigger than just you, Empress.' Amurru shook his head and shuffled away. 'There is much for you to learn from humans.'

She snorted and turned her attention back to David. He had moved across the room to look at the photo of his father. Last night when she had asked David about his father, all he would say was that he was 'missing in action'. She was not sure what that meant, but what did she care? All she wanted was to get unharnessed and back to Genesia as quickly as possible.

David put down the photo and yanked his wardrobe open. He grabbed out more of the boring clothes that he seemed to like. He yanked his old T-shirt off over his head. He had his back to Kora and she could see the muscles ripple with the action.

He hesitated in the process of throwing the discarded top onto the bed. He turned and strode over to her globe.

'Can you see out of there?'

She giggled but didn't answer.

'Kora.' He picked up her globe and gave it a shake. 'Can you see me?'

How dare he shake her globe! She used her magic to cushion Amurru and then shimmered out of her globe in an angry mist of gold.

'Stop that!'

He blinked at her appearance but did stop shaking her globe. 'I asked you a question.'

She realised, now that she was looking at his face, that he was incredibly angry. 'Do not take your petty fight with your mother out on Amurru.'

He looked taken aback and immediately set her globe down. 'Is he okay?'

'Only because I took care of him.'

He turned back to his wardrobe and yanked a clean

T-shirt over his head.

'You can see me.'

She didn't answer.

'Through your globe. You can see out from inside.'

'What does it matter? There is nothing worth looking out at.'

He strode back to tower over her. 'I'm not in the mood for your stuck up royal attitude today.'

'And I am not in the mood for your pathetic human whims.'

'Well, suck it up, Empress,' he snarled. 'Today we are doing things my way.'

She shook her finger at him, the bangles on her arms jingling madly. 'You fool. You have no idea who I am.'

'Actually,' he said. 'I know exactly who you are. You are my slave. And you will do precisely as I command.'

Getting warmer

The front door slammed behind David's mother as she left for work. Kora wondered how long it would take David to summon her. It was less than a second.

'Kora? I wish for you to come outside with me,' he called.

She felt the bands around her wrists and ankles tighten immediately at the command. 'Have a good day, Amurru,' she said. 'I wish I could stay and keep you company.'

Amurru's yellow eyes blinked at her. 'Perhaps today will not be so bad,' he said. She could see compassion in his eyes. 'I know you miss home, Empress.'

She thought sadly of her family. Guilt pierced her heart as she remembered her parting words to her parents. Those few shameful words had played over and over again in her mind ever since. She had told them she hated them.

Amurru seemed to read her thoughts. 'Do not despair, Empress,' he said gently. 'Perhaps I will hear from your father again, soon.'

She nodded. She didn't trust herself to speak. Hopefully Amurru was right. At least then she would know that her family was safe. Her bands were glowing brightly now and dug painfully into her wrists and ankles. She had to go.

'Kora?' David's voice rose in demand. 'Get out here, now!'

She gave Amurru a parting smile and then shimmered gracefully down into David's room. 'You rang, master?'

His eyes narrowed. 'Follow me,' he ordered.

Anger stirred in her chest. How dare he speak to her that way! She stomped into the kitchen behind him.

Cuddles, the ugly, fat ginger cat, lay curled up asleep on one of the kitchen chairs. When Kora entered the room his eyes flew open and, hissing and spitting, he sprang from the chair and fled outside through the cat flap in the back door.

David smirked at her. 'Cuddles really likes you, doesn't he?'

She narrowed her eyes at him. She hated his stupid, sarcastic comments. She folded her arms across her chest and waited.

'Clean up in here.'

She pursed her lips and thought about not doing what he asked. After all, he hadn't really wished for her to do it, but the command was in his voice and she felt her bands tighten. Sighing loudly, she gave in and did what he wanted. In less time than it took for David to blink, the kitchen was spotless.

'In fact,' he said, 'you might as well do the whole house. You can clean the bathrooms, make the beds, do the dusting and vacuum the carpets.' He looked around, frowning. Then he came up with a few more things. 'And clean the windows, mop the floor and put the rubbish out.'

Her anger stirred again but she said nothing. She flicked her hand and did as he had ordered.

David turned and marched outside. Kora stood her ground for as long as she could, but it was only moments before she felt herself being tugged. Not wanting to be dragged out unceremoniously, she followed him outside, cringing as a tidal wave of heat rolled over her. How could it be so hot this early in the day? David was already at the far end of the back yard, slumped on an old garden bench in the shade. With as much dignity as she could muster Kora strode over and stood before him. 'You require something else, master?'

He nodded, one hand swatting at the little swarm of flies that buzzed around his face. He tossed his head, trying to flick back his heavy, long fringe but it just flopped forward again over his eyes. 'I wish for a chocolate milkshake. Double malt and icy cold.'

A tall, silver cup filled with frothy milk appeared on the ground beside him. In seconds, the outside of the cup was covered in glistening drops of condensation that ran down his hand and dripped onto the dry ground. Kora tilted her head to one side and watched him drink, ice cubes clinking against the sides of the cup as he gulped.

It seemed strange to her that a boy like David would just spend each day at home alone. Surely he would need to be educated, or perhaps go out to work? She arched an eyebrow at him. 'Do not Earth children your age have to go to school?'

He shrugged. 'School's out for the summer,' he said. 'Yesterday was the first day of school holidays. That's why my report arrived.' He screwed up his face. 'Boy, I sure wish I had remembered that was coming!' He shook his head in dismay. 'I could have wished for all the Fs to become As before Mum saw it.'

Kora's lip curled. 'Humans are so pathetic,' she said. 'They never want to take responsibility for their actions.'

He glared up at her. Sweat was running down his face and into his eyes, and he wiped it from his brow with the back of his hand. 'You need to get to work,' he said, 'so I can go back inside.'

Kora was cool. A tiny but constant trickle of power around her body shielded her from the heat. But she too wanted to return to the sanctuary of her globe and Amurru. 'Shall we get on with it, then?'

He waved his hand at the mound of firewood. 'Chop that wood into small pieces.'

She nodded and the mound of wood simply vanished, reappearing in small pieces neatly stacked to one side. 'What does your mother want with all this?' she asked. 'No one could need a fire in this disgusting heat!'

'She likes it all to be dried out and ready for winter.' He squinted up at the clear, blue sky. 'It's hard to believe now, but when it gets cold here, it gets cold quickly.'

He turned then and waved towards the chook yard behind him. It seemed even the chickens were feeling the heat. They were clustered up one end of the chook yard where there was a tiny patch of shade, scratching half-heartedly at the barren, dusty ground. 'Clean that out, including their water bowl. And fill up their feed bin.'

She nodded again and the job was done.

He stood and walked over to the back fence where one of the posts had collapsed sideways onto the ground. 'Fix this.' He was standing in the full sun now and fresh beads of sweat sprang out on his face and dripped down his arms.

Kora flicked her fingers at the fence post and it sprang back into place, the dirt compacting around the base of the pole to hold it up.

She folded her arms across her chest and regarded him with her dark eyes. 'Anything else, master?'

'Well, no more chores, at least,' he replied, meeting her gaze. His blue eyes bored into hers for a long moment, making her restless. She knew his slow human brain was coming up with some idiotic idea. Apprehension snaked through her. All she wanted was to return to her globe. She waited for him to speak.

Finally he did. 'Mum will think I spent all day getting those jobs done,' he said, a wide grin spreading across his face. 'And now I've got the rest of the day to do whatever I want.'

She raised an eyebrow at him. 'But surely it is too hot for you to be outside?'

'It might be too hot here,' he said, 'but I know somewhere we can go that's really cool.'

Getting colder

Kora wriggled her toes and sighed with pleasure. She was sitting on a flat, grey rock in the shade of a sprawling weeping willow tree, her bare feet dangling into the clear water of a bubbling creek. She wondered how the water gushing down the tiny creek could be so cold when everything else here was so hot.

She sucked in a long breath and leaned back against the trunk of the tree. She was getting used to the myriad of Earthly smells. At least the damp odour of the rocks and the mouldy leaves that had piled up under the trees was a welcome relief from breathing in the parched air.

'Why don't you join me, Kora?' David's voice was muffled by the sound of the water cascading around him.

'No, thank you,' she replied, gazing across the creek to where he reclined under a little waterfall. The water crashed down onto the top of his head and streamed down his bare chest and shoulders. Kora tipped her head sideways to study him. He certainly had broad shoulders. His arms were tanned a dark, golden brown, but the pale white skin on his chest in the shape of his T-shirt made her smile. Humans were truly strange creatures.

He had been in the water for nearly an hour now and she could see goose bumps appearing along his arms. She supposed having to chop wood and mend fences without magic would give someone muscles that rippled like David's did. He pushed his dripping hair back out of his eyes and she saw that the skin on his hands had wrinkled from being in the water too long.

Abruptly she realised that David was watching her watching him and she dropped her eyes back to the water. 'How far from Panda Rock are we?' she asked.

'Not far,' he said, waving vaguely off to his left. 'It's about a kilometre that way.'

'You know, I still have not seen the panda-shaped mountain.'

He pushed himself up out of the creek. 'We can go see it now if you like,' he said, picking up his dry T-shirt and pulling it on over his head. 'We only need to walk a little way.' He shook his head vigorously like a dog and droplets of water flew in every direction, splattering her.

She leaned away from the flying droplets and David grinned. 'We can get a great view of Panda Rock from down there,' he said, pointing down the hill through the trees. 'The angle's just right and you can see the entire outline of the bear.'

'I would like that.' She followed David, ducking under branches and weaving between the trees. As they emerged from the shade into the bright sunlight the familiar wall of heat greeted them. Kora immediately channelled a tiny trickle of magic to protect herself. But it seemed only seconds before David's wet hair and shorts had dried and droplets of sweat were dripping down his face.

They trudged down to the base of the slope. Kora turned and gazed up at the strangely shaped hill. It looked as though the rocks had tumbled down out of the sky, piling awkwardly up one on top of the other, to form the unlikely shape of a panda.

'It is beautiful, David.'

The rocks rounded out from the base to form the panda's rotund belly, skimmed back in on themselves to form a much thinner neck, and then curved smoothly out again to create the shape of a panda's chubby, cute face.

'And see,' said David, pointing up towards the panda's head. 'It's smiling.'

'So it is,' Kora replied, smiling herself. The deep fissures in the rocks curved around the base of the panda's face creating the illusion of a serene smile. 'I did not expect it to look quite so much like a real panda.'

When she finally glanced back at David, she found him eyeing her thoughtfully. 'How come you're not sweating?' he asked. His own hair was clumped in sweaty strands down the sides of his face. His eyes narrowed at her. 'Are you using magic to keep cool?'

'Yes.' She smiled smugly. 'But for a weather shield to work it must attach to a person, and you know I cannot use magic on a human.'

David's brow furrowed. She waited, one eyebrow raised. She could see he was trying to think of a way to get what he wanted. Then his eyes lit up, his face triumphant.

He looked convinced that he had somehow beaten her at her own game. 'Kora,' he ordered, his voice smug. 'I wish for a fresh, cool breeze to blow on me.'

A twist of fear shot through her. 'No, David!' But the command had been clear and specific. Her bands glowed as she resisted the order. 'Unwish it, David,' she pleaded. 'It's dangerous.'

The power grew steadily in her chest and her bands tightened. 'David, please,' she begged. 'Quickly.' But he didn't speak. He just stared dumbly at her as she battled against the wish. She couldn't hold out much longer against it. Her power rumbled, mingling with the fear twisting through her. Her body arched with the pain of resisting.

'David!' she screamed. She was vaguely aware of him standing frozen, gaping at her. Stupid, slow-reacting humans! She could no longer contain the power and it surged from her chest in a torrent. At once the nearby trees bent over in the wind and the leaves and dust stirred off the ground and swirled around their feet.

The breeze was cool and strong and David's long hair lifted off his face as it flowed over him. Perhaps it was this burst of fresh, cold air that finally brought him to his senses. 'I wish for the wind to stop,' he blurted quickly. And as suddenly as it began, it vanished. Immediately the heavy, oppressive heat pressed down on them once more.

Exhausted from the battle against her own magic, Kora could barely stand. She bent over at the waist, resting her hands on her knees, and blew out a long, unsteady breath.

David tipped his head to one side as he contemplated her.

She remained hunched over, panting with the pain and effort of resisting his command.

She didn't look up but she could feel his penetrating blue gaze as he studied her.

'Kora?'

She lifted her dark eyes wearily. 'What?'

He dragged a shaky hand through his hair. 'What just happened?'

Run!

The heat was overwhelming. Without the use of her magic, sweat ran freely down her back and dripped across her forehead.

'Can't I have just one wish?' David called back to her.

'No, no magic,' she panted. 'Just run!'

David's long legs carried him much faster than hers possibly could. Her heart thumped in her chest and she could feel her pulse pounding in her ears. She twisted her head around to scan behind them and tripped, landing face first in the scorching hot dirt.

She heard his footsteps make their way back to her.

'Here,' he was breathing hard. 'Take my hand.'

She pushed the long dark hair that stuck to her face away to glare at him. This was all his stupid fault. But she accepted his hand and allowed him to pull her to her feet. He kept hold of her hand. Half-running, half-dragging her along with him, she tried her best to keep up. It felt like they had been running for hours, not minutes. Her knees were cut from the fall and a thin trickle of blood oozed down her leg.

'Are we safe yet?' David asked raggedly.

'No!' Kora yanked her hand from his and stopped for a moment. She put her hands on her hips and leaned forward. Breathing hard, she wondered if she was actually going to be sick.

David's eyes searched the landscape. 'Can we hide somewhere here?'

She shook her head but soon stopped as the ground spun dizzily. 'Not far enough away yet.'

He grasped her hand tightly. 'Come on, then.'

He set a gruelling pace. Her legs scrambled numbly after him. She had never relied on her physical body this way before. She had never needed to and it made her feel vulnerable. Weak. Her mouth was dry and her lungs ached. They had come a long way but she knew it was still not far enough.

She could feel herself getting humiliatingly slower. David was dragging her more than she was running. Her arm no longer felt as if it belonged to her and she wondered if he had pulled it from its socket.

'I can see the house.' David's speed increased despite the fact that they were now headed uphill. Her legs gave way from under her and she fell again to the ground. Her sweaty hand slipped out of David's grasp and she rolled until she landed shoulder first against a hard sharp rock. Pain pierced through her.

'Kora?' David was bending over her. 'Are you all right?'

She couldn't speak at first. 'My shoulder,' she finally croaked.

'Can we use your magic now?'

'Not yet.' She bit down on her lip and tried to push herself up, but before she knew it David's hands were under her and she was swung up onto his back.

'What are you doing?'

'What does it look like I'm doing?' He wound his arms so that his hands gripped tightly to her legs, holding her in place on his back. 'I'm giving you a piggyback. Try to hang on.'

She pushed against him but that just made the shooting pain in her shoulder worse. 'Put me down.'

He was already taking long strides up the hill. 'No.'

'I am too heavy for you to carry.'

His skin was already reddened from heat and now it darkened further with the exertion of carrying her. 'I'll manage,' he said. 'I'm human.'

Exhausted and sick with pain she gave up. She doubted she would be able to make the rest of the way to the house relying on just her own physical body. How did humans live like this, every day with no magic?

Breathing hard, he made no attempt to speak to her but his pace never slowed. He made his way, dripping with sweat, face set in determined lines, steadily and surely towards the house.

He let go of her leg to push open the front door and then kicked it closed behind them. 'What now?' he rasped.

'Wish us into my globe.'

The moment he wished she closed her eyes and very carefully, using the most minuscule amount of magic possible, they shimmered.

The pirate

Amurru shuffled out of one of the darkened corners of
her globe. 'What has happened, Empress?' He glanced at
David then back to her. 'You are hurt?'

She was slumped on David's back, her head over one
shoulder. 'Set me down.'

He looked bewildered but swung her carefully off his
back and onto a bed of gold cushions. 'Is it safe now?'

Amurru's ears twitched but his yellow eyes stayed fixed
on her. 'Why do you not use your magic to heal yourself,
Empress?'

'Idiot here wished for a cool wind.' She threw a
scornful look at David, but then felt bad when she saw the
lines of exhaustion that etched his face.

Amurru's head drooped. 'This is grave.'

'We are safe now, aren't we?' David slumped down on
the floor of her globe. 'We didn't use any magic.'

She ignored him. Stupid, idiotic, clueless human! Her

power rumbled around inside her.

Amurru's head jerked up. 'Control, Empress.'

She took a steadying breath. 'Yes, you are right.' She closed her eyes for a moment and then, using the smallest amount of power that she could, she made a viewing portal appear.

'That's Panda Rock.' David stepped nearer to the viewing portal. 'What are all those people doing there?'

'Not people,' she said. 'Genies.'

'So many.' Amurru's voice filled with sadness. 'He has harnessed even more in the last two days.'

'Rihando looks miserable.'

'He is very loyal to your family.' Amurru shuffled himself over until he was almost touching her. 'This would be killing him.'

'Are you talking about that bigger one in the red coat, or the one that looks like a mad pirate?'

'The red coat,' said Kora. 'The mad pirate is Vennum.'

Vennum turned in their direction. He had dark oily hair and wild, crazed eyes. His disfigured arms were gesturing madly revealing purple scars and fresh welts that crisscrossed their way up and down his flesh.

'Do you think Vennum knows it was you at Panda Rock?' asked David.

The sound coming through to them was a jumble of

angry voices. Amurru's ears twitched. 'They are not sure. They are arguing amongst themselves.'

David paced her globe. 'Are we safe in here?'

'I do not know.' She let out a sigh. 'But we did not leave a magic trail for them to follow.'

'You did well to not wish for anything during your escape,' said Amurru. 'Otherwise Vennum would have killed you by now.'

David swallowed. 'And this is all my fault?' He looked unsure. 'Because I wished for a cool wind?'

'Vennum was monitoring Earth for the use of excessive power.'

'And a cool wind would take a lot of power?'

'Any control of the elements would show as a power spike.'

'It is fortunate it was only a breeze, Empress.' Amurru's focus was still on the conversation outside. 'They cannot now be sure that it was you.'

'What does he mean? How would they know it was you? Couldn't it have been any genie?' asked David.

'Most genies can summon a breeze, that is why they are uncertain.' She looked him in the eyes. 'How much the elements are controlled shows how powerful the genie is.'

'So if I had wished for a hurricane, Vennum would know it was you?'

'Yes.'

'Because yours would be so fierce?'

Her eyes glittered. 'Because I am the most powerful genie on Genesia.'

'If you are the most powerful genie then can't you use your magic to stop them if they find us?'

'I will try. But I am one genie against many.' She gestured towards the viewing portal.

'Why don't you just kill him?'

'I wish. But it simply is not possible for a genie to kill a human.' She scowled at Vennum through the portal. 'And Vennum is human enough that it includes him!'

David breathed in through his nose and dropped his arms to his side. 'I'm sorry, Kora.'

His apology surprised her. Genies were seldom sorry for anything and certainly never said so.

'If Vennum finds me, wish yourself to a hiding spot and then wish me unharnessed.' She sighed. 'I should be able to hold them off long enough for you to run.'

'But then Vennum could harness you. Can't you just magic us all away now?'

'They would notice and follow any use of magic.'

'What about that?' David pointed at the viewing portal. 'Doesn't that leave a trail?'

'I am using a tiny amount of magic. If there were only

one genie out there, they would probably be able to detect it. But because there are so many of them, and they are quite a distance away, it is not strong enough for them to be able to notice that it is not coming from one of them.'

David began to pace her globe. 'So every time you use magic it leaves a trail?'

'Yes, but the trail disappears after a while.'

'And Vennum can see the trail?'

'Not see it. Sense it. And not Vennum, but his genies.'

'So if the trail we would have left going to Panda Rock has disappeared,' David kept pacing, 'and we didn't use any magic to get back, and they didn't see us, then we should be safe, right?'

'Maybe.' Kora huffed. 'I wish they would stop yelling at each other. I cannot tell what they are saying.'

Amurru's ear turned and his face wrinkled with concentration. 'Rihando has told Vennum that whatever genie was here has gone but Vennum has found your footprints and wants to follow them.'

She looked at the human. He had carried her over a kilometre up a hill, and then apologised to her. She may not be fond of humans but she would no longer like to see him dead. 'If they come, David, unharness me.'

He folded his arms. 'No.'

'I am powerful and Vennum will kill you.'

'I know you don't think much of me.' She saw the anger flood his face. 'But I am not about to leave you, powerful or not, to face that slimeball alone.'

She stared back at his angry eyes. What was he thinking? That he was going to be able to protect her from Vennum? Her mind raced as she tried to come up with a plan. She would not be able to hold that many genies off for long.

She felt Amurru stiffen beside her. 'Vennum is decided, Empress. He intends to follow the tracks.'

She reached out and placed a hand on his shoulder. 'If the time comes, Amurru. Will you tell my family that I love them?' She glanced up at David. 'And tell my parents,' she stumbled over the aching in her throat, 'tell them I am sorry.'

Amurru's short stumpy fingers rested on her hand. 'You have my word, Empress.'

David squared his shoulders. 'They're headed this way!'

Tracks

David burst out laughing.

She looked at him in disbelief. What was wrong with him? 'I am glad your imminent death amuses you.'

'I don't suppose genies spend much time hunting.' David pointed at the viewing portal. The genies were spreading out now, splashing around in the creek and pointing at the ground. 'They're not our tracks.'

'He is right, Empress. They cannot agree on a direction.' Amurru's ears swivelled, slowly making sense of the jumbled, shouting voices coming through the portal. 'They fight amongst themselves again.'

She blew out a long slow breath. Her shoulder was excruciating and her knees were bloody and sore. When her eyes landed on David she could see the dark red stain that covered his shirt where her shoulder had been pressed against him.

She watched Vennum in the viewing portal. His arms

were flapping madly and pure rage emanated from him. A sword appeared in his hand and in a movement too fast to follow he whirled around, slicing the blade across the face of the nearest genie, leaving a long, ragged, bloody slash. The genie let out a bloodcurdling scream, flinging his hands up to cover the gaping wound on his face. Then, with a final roar of rage, Vennum and the genies all disappeared, and the forest fell silent.

'What happened?' Kora looked to Amurru. 'And what was Vennum yelling about?'

'He was furious that they could not follow the tracks. And he has ordered them to keep a close eye on this area.'

David got to his feet. 'How will they do that?'

'They will continue to watch for even the smallest of power spikes,' said Amurru. 'You must both be careful.'

She shifted painfully against the pillows. 'He really means you need to be more careful.'

David ignored the jab. 'Where do you keep your bandages?'

'Why, are you hurt?'

'No, but you are.'

'Not for long.' She settled herself and closed her eyes. First she directed her magic to her shoulder, and when that was blissfully painfree she directed it down to her knees and then finally around her aching, sore muscles.

She opened her eyes to find his fascinated gaze on her. 'That was amazing.'

'No. What is amazing,' she said, raising one dark eyebrow, 'is how you can bear to live without magic.'

'So you never stay hurt or get sick?'

'Mostly we heal ourselves.'

'What do you mean "mostly"?'

'We have to be conscious to channel our power to where it is needed.'

'So what happens if you're unconscious?'

'Then we have a problem.'

'So you just have to hope you become conscious in time to heal yourself?'

'Pretty much.'

'Can't another genie heal you?'

'No, it does not work that way. You have to be able to guide your own magic to where you need it. But if things are desperate enough another genie can take you to the Slaytians for help.'

'Who are the Slaytians?'

'You ask a lot of questions. Are you not tired?'

He shrugged and waited expectantly.

She sighed. 'They are forest-dwelling creatures that live in the Genesian wilderness. They are similar looking in some ways to genies and humans, but they are smaller and have green skin. Most importantly, though, they have rather unusual powers.'

'They can heal, too?'

'Yes. They have powerful concoctions made from ingredients harvested from the forest. But they heal genies in a different way. This talent is more subtle. They can invade your mind in a way that leaves you uncertain which thoughts are your own and which thoughts they have put there. Useful if you are unconscious because they can make your mind direct your magic.' She raised her eyebrows. 'Not so useful the rest of the time.'

Her throat was still dry and her mouth felt sticky. She flicked her wrist and produced cold fruit drinks for them both.

David raised his glass and took a huge gulp. He was grimy and sweaty. 'So this means I can make wishes again now?'

She rolled her eyes and nodded. That would be right. Typical human boy, straight back to thinking about himself.

'So why don't the Slaytians use their mind trick on Vennum?'

'My father has asked them, but the Slaytians are not our friends.'

'That's a surprise.'

Her head jerked up at his sarcastic tone. 'You know nothing of us.'

'But I'm learning. So why aren't the Slaytians and genies friends?'

She shrugged. 'It is complicated.'

'Then why do they bother to heal you?'

'They do not do so for free.'

'Surely a genie would pay any price to get rid of Vennum?'

'The Slaytians are power-hungry. My father refused to exchange one evil power for another.'

David began to pace her globe again, this time in interest. 'I wondered what it would be like in here.' His eyes roved around, taking in the colourful floating lamps, the sparkling silken fabrics and the panoramic viewing screens showing the outside world and the inside of his bedroom. He sucked in his breath and jabbed his finger at the screens. 'I knew you could see me from in here!'

Kora grinned. 'Of course. What did you expect?'

David reached up to touch one of the tiny floating lamps. 'I didn't expect the inside of your globe to look like this!'

'Really?' asked Kora. 'Well then, did you expect this?' She waved her hand and the inside of her globe transformed into the deck of an old-fashioned ship, complete with wooden decking, and captain's bridge with oversized steering wheel.

David laughed, and stepped over to take the wheel. 'Land ahoy,' he yelled.

Kora flicked her fingers. A wave appeared over the bow of the ship and dumped sea water on David's head.

He spluttered, and plucked a long strand of brown seaweed from his face. But before he could complain, she waved her hand again and the ship's deck and sea water disappeared, leaving a dripping David standing in the middle of a colourful lolly shop.

'Or maybe you expected it to look like this?' All around were jars, bowls and bottles of chocolates and lollies of every shape and size.

David gaped at the display, before stepping over and grabbing a handful of Smarties.

'That's incredible,' he mumbled around a mouthful of the lollies. 'So it just looks however you want it to?'

Kora nodded. 'Pretty much.'

He reached out to a bowl of false teeth lollies, shoved one in his mouth, and bared his new fangs at her.

Kora sighed loudly. He was so juvenile. 'Do you not want to leave now?'

He seemed to enjoy her irritation. 'I've got plenty of time.'

'How can you tell?' she scoffed. 'I know that stupid watch of yours does not even work.'

David's face closed over at her words. 'You're right,' he said in a flat voice. 'I do want to leave. Now!'

A night at the movies

Kora leaned back with a contented sigh against the silk cushions and settled in to watch David's family dinner on the viewing portal suspended in front of her. Her bangles jingled as she curled her arm around a glass bowl full of hot, buttery popcorn.

Amurru huffed. 'You think this is an entertainment event, Empress?'

Kora grinned. Amurru's voice was disapproving but she could see the glint of humour in his round, yellow eyes. 'Absolutely!' She gracefully nibbled at a ball of popcorn. 'I wonder if all Earth families are as funny?'

Amurru nodded. 'I think that may be the case, Empress.' He shuffled over to his chair and clambered awkwardly into it. 'I have heard that humans are all very different from each other.' He coughed out a wheezy laugh. 'And David's family certainly supports that theory.'

Kora grimaced. 'Eeewww, Amurru. Look what they are eating! It is disgusting.'

'It is not what I imagined humans would eat,' he agreed.

She watched fascinated as Rodney scooped large piles of sloppy brown stew onto each plate. 'Thanks,' mumbled David. He took his plate and inspected the contents.

Kora gagged. 'It looks like vomit!'

Amurru's ears twitched. 'Perhaps it tastes better than it looks, Empress?'

She shook her head vehemently. 'I doubt it, Amurru.' She screwed her face up in horror as Marcia placed a lump of some kind of green, slimy vegetable onto the plate next to the slop. 'You did not smell the tofu pasta they had for dinner last night!'

'Here we go,' sang Marcia. 'Doesn't this look interesting?'

'Yeah, it's interesting all right.' David's voice was hardly audible as he mumbled down into his plate. He began to poke at his dinner with his fork.

'It's a new recipe I'm trialling for my shop,' said Rodney. 'I want to expand my range. I thought it would be good to sell some ready-to-eat lines, as well as the usual health food items.'

Kora had to look away as Rodney shoved the goo into his mouth.

Amurru scratched at the tuft of hair between his pointy ears. 'I find it fascinating that he calls it health food, Empress,' he wheezed. 'Especially when he does not look particularly healthy.'

She took a closer look. Amurru was right. Rodney had pale, blotchy skin that he was forever scratching, and puffy, red eyes as though he never got enough sleep. Even Marcia looked tired and pale, and tonight Kora could see she also had dark rings around her eyes. Perhaps neither of them had slept well.

'Do you like it, David?' Marcia smiled encouragingly.

'Well …' His voice trailed off and he stared into space. Kora had already come to know this look. David was thinking of something.

'What is he doing?' asked Amurru.

Kora shrugged. 'Probably coming up with another of his hair-brained ideas.'

David's eyes sharpened and he spoke, very loudly. 'It's not bad, Mum,' he said, turning his head so that his voice would carry down the passage and into his room. 'But I wish it tasted like a hamburger and chips.'

'That's ridiculous, David,' replied his mother. 'You know how unhealthy it is to eat such junk.' She clicked her tongue at him. 'And there's no need to shout at the dinner table.'

Kora glanced at Amurru. At David's wish her bands had tightened and were now glowing a soft, golden yellow.

Amurru blinked knowingly at her. 'The boy learns, Empress.'

She laughed as she channelled her magic out to the kitchen. 'Yes. I just hope he continues to think carefully before he makes his wishes.'

David shovelled a forkful of the slop into his mouth. 'I can honestly say it tastes great, Rodney.'

Rodney's cheeks glowed bright red with pleasure as David scooped another huge forkful into his mouth.

Marcia swallowed her own mouthful of food. 'You know, David, I really appreciate all the extra chores you did today.'

He shrugged. 'It's no problem, Mum.'

'I realise you must have worked for most of the day to get so much done.'

David looked at his mother. 'I had nothing else to do. Not now that I'm grounded.'

Marcia put her fork down and narrowed her eyes. 'You know, it's not that I don't appreciate all your hard work,' she said. 'But if you think it changes how I feel about your poor performance at school this year, you're wrong.'

David's brow creased as he stared back down at his food, but he didn't answer. His heavy, long fringe dropped forward over his face, hiding his eyes.

Marcia took a deep breath and changed the subject. 'What time do you finish work tomorrow, David?'

'Twelve o'clock,' he replied.

'Good,' she said, nodding. 'Then make sure you get a haircut before you come home.'

David's eyes stayed glued to his plate. He lifted one shoulder in a half shrug.

'I mean it, David,' said Marcia, her voice rising a little.

Rodney reached out and patted her arm. 'Don't worry, dear,' he said, throwing David a smile. 'I'm sure David will get his hair cut straight after work.'

David lifted his eyes to glare at Rodney. Kora was surprised. She hadn't realised there was any antagonism between them.

Marcia sighed and reached across the table to gather the empty plates together. 'We can talk more about that later,' she said. 'For now, David, there's something else we need to discuss with you.'

Kora heard the quiver in Marcia's voice and wondered what was making her nervous. She glanced at Amurru. He must have heard it too. His ears flicked forwards and his eyes were trained on the portal.

David put down his fork. 'Yeah?' he asked, suspicion making his voice raspy.

Rodney smiled warmly at him. 'Your mother and I have decided to move in together.'

'What?' David's mouth dropped open in shock. 'What do you mean, move in together?' His eyes jerked to his mother's face and then back to Rodney's. 'And live where?' His voice rose shakily. 'Not here?'

'Now, David, calm down,' said his mother. 'I know it may take you some time to get used to the idea, but it will be for the best.'

'For the best? How can you say that?' David glared at his mother. 'When is he moving in?'

'This weekend.'

'And what about Dad?' yelled David. 'What about when Dad comes home?'

Marcia sighed. 'Now, that's exactly why it is for the best,' she said, her voice gentle. 'Rodney and I thought it might be best for you … that is, I mean to say …' Her voice cracked and broke. She smoothed her blond pony tail nervously. Taking a deep breath, she plunged on. 'The truth is we thought it might be nice for you to have a father figure in the house.' She smiled nervously at Rodney as she spoke.

Rodney's face was a picture of compassion as he nodded at David. 'Your mother thinks it might help you accept that your father isn't coming back.' He reached his hand out to pat David's arm.

David jerked his arm out of Rodney's reach. His chair scraped violently against the floor. 'How can you say that?'

'David, please. Be reasonable.' Marcia reached her hand out towards him.

David stared numbly at her for a long, long moment. Then his voice dropped to a whisper. 'You don't know, Mum.' He shook his head in disbelief and despair. 'You don't know he isn't coming back.' David glanced at Rodney and then turned his burning blue gaze back to his mother. 'How could you do this to Dad?'

Marcia stood silently gazing back at him, her eyes full of sadness and pain until David turned and left the room.

Kora's eyes met Amurru's. 'I had no idea.'

He nodded. 'There is much we have to learn about humans.' His round, yellow eyes blinked at her. 'Especially your human.'

She wiggled her fingers and the portal vanished. She could hear David clomping down the passage. 'I wonder if I should go out and see him?'

Amurru stood. His great yellow eyes seemed to cloud over for a moment. When they focused again he bowed his head to her. 'I have been summoned, Empress.'

Storm clouds

Kora woke abruptly.

'You dreamt again, Empress?'

'Yes.' She would never admit it but she was glad of Amurru's company.

'The same as the night before?'

She nodded. Her father had summoned Amurru on Friday night. Vennum's power had increased significantly. Extra guards had been placed around her little brother, and the castle was on highest alert. Of course Amurru had told her father about her close call with Vennum. Amurru said her father had merely been anxious for her safety but she knew Amurru well enough to suspect that her father had been furious and had most likely vented that anger on him.

'They are just dreams, Empress.' Amurru's yellow eyes rested on her. 'It is natural for you to be worried.'

Worried. What a small word to describe all that she

was feeling. She sighed, and conjured up breakfast for them.

Amurru sipped his juice. 'Perhaps David will summon you out of your globe today.'

She, too, wondered if David would be in a better mood today. The dinner on Friday night had gone from bad to worse for him. After being told that Rodney was moving in, David's boss had rung and told his mother that he was sacked from his job. He worked at an electrical store in Panda Rock and his mate Hammer had been caught by the police with stolen goods from the shop. His boss believed that David had known about the theft and had kept it a secret to protect his friend. Rodney had then questioned again all the prizes he claimed to have won in the raffle.

It had all unravelled terribly for David after that. His mother, ranting and waving her hands, had taken away his phone and his iPod and everything else she could lay her hands on. She had looked like a madwoman. When Kora had shimmered into his room after his mother had left she had offered to replace all the things his mother had taken but David had simply shaken his head and wished that she would get lost back into her globe. He hadn't summoned her since.

'Maybe,' she said. 'But for now he has wished me to stay in here.'

Amurru's ears twitched madly. 'I think David's mother has something in mind for him.'

Kora stopped to listen. David had left his bedroom a few minutes earlier. She couldn't quite make out his mother's words but David's grunt of reply was followed by the loud slam of his bedroom door.

'Kora!'

'I am summoned.' She flashed a smile at Amurru and shimmered out of her globe, happy to have something else to temporarily occupy her thoughts.

David looked as miserable as he had on Friday night. 'We have to go to the shops,' he said.

'Do you wish me to take you there?'

'Nah, we'll walk. It's about two kilometres, but the longer I'm out of this house the better. You should probably magic up some normal clothes. Meet me at the front gate.'

With a quick flick of her wrist she was wearing jeans and a T-shirt, and she shimmered outside to meet David.

They walked in silence. Kora felt sorry for David but his black mood was getting tiresome. The weather had changed, too. Clouds gathered in the previously blue sky and the air was hot and sticky. The humidity strengthened the disgusting Earth smell and it took a constant stream of magic to make this unwelcoming environment bearable.

'What's your mum like?' His question caught her by surprise. 'Bet she's not as crazed as mine.'

'Just her hair.'

'What?'

'She has crazy hair.' She used her magic to transform her own hair into a replica of her mother's.

David burst out laughing. 'Are you for real?'

'Totally.' She changed back to her own hair. 'Aside from that she is very calm and controlled.' She grinned. 'Fury runs more on my father's side of the family.'

'Not hard to tell who you take after, then.'

They walked along the quiet road passing houses similar to David's.

'Do all humans live this far apart from each other?'

David frowned at her. 'What do you mean?'

'Your houses are quite far apart from each other.' She pointed at the passing homes. 'It seems a lot of space for a few humans.'

'Well, it depends where you live.' David half smiled. 'Panda Rock is in the hills.' He pointed towards the west. 'The closer you get to Perth the closer people live to one another.'

They reached a corner and turned left. 'What's that?'

she asked, pointing to a large cluster of buildings.

'Prison.'

It didn't look like much of a prison, but then she guessed they were only humans.

David let out a bark of laughter. 'I'm kidding. It's Panda Rock Senior High School.'

'It looks less like a school than it does a prison.'

'You go to school, then?'

'Yes, all genies go to school until they are sixteen. I attend The Academy of Power Mastery.'

'That sounds a lot more fun than Panda High.' They had reached the front of the school where she could now see a tired sign with the school name on it. Directly opposite was a shop. 'You should probably wait here.'

David went on ahead. The clouds that filled the sky were getting thicker and darker and Kora wondered if she would see her first Earth rain.

Within a couple of minutes David came out of the deli just as a teenage girl and boy walked toward the shop. She saw David stop. Even from across the road she could see he was angry.

The boy was skinny with a bulging forehead covered in zits, and two thin, blond rat's tails that hung down his back. But the girl he had his arm around was pretty, with green eyes that matched her strappy top and brown curly hair that was pulled up in a ponytail.

Kora used her magic to eavesdrop on what they were saying.

'Where have you been?' the boy asked David. 'I've been calling you all weekend.'

David stared at the girl and then shifted his focus to the boy. She could see the cold blue glare David was giving him. 'You can't answer a phone if you don't have one.' He poked the boy in the chest. 'And thanks to you, Hammer, I don't have a job any more, either!'

'Take it easy, mate.' Hammer unhooked his arm from around the girl and held his hands up in surrender. 'I didn't mean to cause you any grief.'

'You're not my mate!' David's glare shifted from Hammer to the girl. 'And we only broke up two weeks ago, Tiffany.'

'That's right,' said Hammer. 'Broke up!'

David gave Hammer a hard shove in the chest sending him flying backwards onto the ground. The shopping bag in David's hand swung around wildly. 'You deserve each other,' he spat.

Then he turned his back on them and crossed the road in quick angry strides.

Hammer picked himself up off the ground but didn't follow him. 'Guess the camping trip is off, then?'

David spared them one last glance. 'Get stuffed,' he said, and strode right past Kora and down the road.

It's raining

David was walking away so fast that Kora could feel the tug on her bands. He must have noticed too because he finally stopped and waited for her to catch up.

'So I guess that was Hammer and Tiffany?' she said when she reached him.

'I don't want to talk about it.'

'The girl was very pretty.'

David glared at her. 'I wish,' he said, 'not to talk about Hammer and Tiffany.'

She shrugged. What did she care about his stupid human friends? She looked instead down at the small bag he held. 'So we walked all this way for that?'

'Ty the Spy doesn't drink soy milk.'

'Who the what?'

'Ty the Spy. Rodney's daughter.' He let out a huge sigh. 'She's coming for lunch today.'

That explained a lot. 'You do not like her?'

'Tyra's okay. It's the spy part that's the problem.'

'A spy?' Kora frowned.

'Yep, and she's got all the gear. Night vision binoculars, eavesdropping devices, voice recorders. It goes on and on.'

'You will have to be careful that I am not discovered while she is spying on you, David.'

David raised an eyebrow. 'You mean we will have to be careful.'

'I am always careful.' Kora glanced at him. 'Now that Rodney lives with you, does that mean she will be around a lot?'

David groaned. 'I really hope not.'

Lapsing into silence, they made their way back toward home. After his earlier speed he now walked so slowly that for once her shorter legs could easily keep pace with him.

After a while David spoke again. 'Do you think Vennum is still watching Panda Rock?'

'He will not give up looking for me.' She frowned. 'Rihando would do his best to keep me from Vennum, but because he is harnessed there is little he can really do to help me.'

'Rihando, that was the big genie with Vennum?'

'Yes, in the red coat. He was our most trusted and loyal genie.'

'Vennum harnessed him?'

'Yes, about five years ago. We are not sure how Vennum managed to do so. We were all devastated when we found out. My father has not been the same since.'

'What about Amurru?' asked David. 'Why is he here?'

'Armourowls and genies have a long history and Amurru has served my family for many centuries.'

'Was Amurru in danger, too? Is that why he came with you?'

'All of Genesia is in danger.' She glanced at him, wondering if the questions were genuine interest or a way of distracting himself from his own problems. 'His purpose for me here is his projection. Armourowls can project themselves to another place. It enables me to receive communication from home. Although I suspect my father is using it the other way around.'

They had reached the hill that led back up to the house and David slowed down even more. 'But Amurru also has his own kind of magic.'

David's head whipped up. 'Can he grant wishes, too?'

'Do you think of nothing else?' She let out an exasperated sigh. 'Armourowls' magic is very mysterious. They cannot conjure items but they can exert an influence over creatures and events. We call it "Creation Magic". They have a way of making things happen.'

'Does Creation Magic work on you?' asked David.

'Can they influence you to do things?'

'Unfortunately, yes. And it is most annoying that the same does not apply to them.'

'What do you mean?'

'Like you, David, armourowls are impervious to genie magic.'

'He's such a funny little creature with those big, orange wings.' David smiled. 'Can he actually fly?'

'Not very well and not very far. But do not be deceived,' warned Kora. 'Armourowls are not as fragile as they look. Amurru, though, is very old even for an armourowl, and I know his leg pains him.'

'What happened to his leg?'

'He was badly wounded protecting my grandmother when they were out in the Genesian wilderness. But that was very long ago when Amurru was still young.'

'Just how old is he?'

'He celebrated his 1173rd birthday two weeks before we left Genesia. At that point in time there was not any mention of the possibility that he would come to Earth with me.'

'Do genies usually come to Earth alone?'

'If they are banished to Earth as a punishment they come alone, but a royal genie would always bring an armourowl.' She smoothed a hand along her sleek hair.

'Amurru's nephew, Tarru, was meant to travel with me.'

'So, why didn't he? Surely a younger armourowl would be better protection for you?'

'That is a very good question and it makes me suspicious, because armourowls always have a reason for everything they do.' She sighed. 'But no matter how much I think about it, I have not been able to imagine any reason for Amurru to have chosen to risk what might be the last years of his life stuck here on Earth with me.'

She could see David putting it together. 'So if something happens to Amurru while you are on Earth you won't be able to communicate with your family?'

'Correct.'

'I can't believe your parents allowed that. You could be here for years.'

'They trust him.'

'How about you?' asked David. 'Do you trust him?'

'He is secretive, sneaky and manipulative, but for all that, yes, I trust him.' She sighed. 'But that does not mean I will always like what he does or how he does it.'

'Are there a lot of armourowls on Genesia?'

'Their numbers are growing. Like us, they usually live to be around a thousand years old. And they can have more children than genies can.'

'What do you mean?' David looked surprised. 'Can't

you have many kids?'

'We can only have children during a very short period of our lives. Most genies are happy if they are able to have two children.'

The wind had picked up. She could see it in the way it made David's shaggy hair blow across his face. It was nearly midday but the dark sky made it feel much later. She saw him glance at his broken watch.

'You know I could fix that for you.'

'No, thanks.' He smiled but it didn't quite reach his eyes. 'I like it the way it is.'

She shrugged. 'Suit yourself.'

They had reached the fence outside the house. David groaned as they spied Rodney's bike leaning against the house alongside a smaller bike with a pink and white spotted helmet hanging from its handlebars. White lace curtains flapped out of the open kitchen window. As they watched, a small, blond head poked out the window under the curtain and trained a pair of binoculars down the street.

The wind carried the scent of something that didn't smell like anything anyone should have to eat.

'Mum's cooking nut roast,' said David.

She wrinkled her nose. 'I bet I can guess your next wish.'

David rubbed his hand across his broken watch and when he spoke his voice was serious. 'Actually, I've been thinking a lot about wishes and there is something I want to talk to you about.'

The sky was very black now and thunder rumbled around them. 'What is it?'

A bolt of lightning cracked overhead, the bright flash making them both jump, and then big fat drops of rain began to fall.

He lifted his face toward the sky and let the rain run down his face. They both turned to the sound of the kitchen door banging and saw Rodney on the verandah peering out into the rain.

David sighed. 'Guess it'll have to wait.' He was getting wetter by the second while she stood dry inside the cocoon of her weather shield.

A wicked grin flashed across his face. 'I wish for you to get wet,' he blurted out with a laugh and then ran off splashing through the mud, leaving her soaked through, her hair plastered to her face, and a long string of profanities running through her head.

Missing in action

David stretched out in Kora's globe, a large bowl of hot chips cradled in his lap. 'Ah, peace and quiet, at last.' He leaned his head back against the wall and closed his eyes.

Kora studied David as he rested. He looked tired, his face pale and drawn. But she had no intention of letting him fall asleep in her globe. She had only brought him in here so they could talk without risk of being overheard. She pursed her lips thoughtfully and waited to see if his eyes opened again. But his breathing only grew deeper. The bowl of chips on his lap tilted precariously, forgotten, and she waved it down to the floor beside him.

She let her eyes travel over his face. It seemed softer somehow, the hard lines of his mouth and forehead gentling as he relaxed against the cushions. She breathed out a long sigh. The last few days had been a stressful time.

David's thick black lashes quivered unexpectedly

against the paler skin of his cheeks, drawing her gaze, and she knew he was falling asleep.

'So, David,' she said loudly, leaning back against her own cushions, 'Ty the Spy finally went home?'

'Yeah, and not a moment too soon.' David pushed himself back up into a sitting position. 'You must have noticed the silence in the house after she left?'

Kora laughed. 'She did have a lot of questions for you today.' She thought of the girl's cute freckled face as she had rattled off question after question at David, tossing her ponytail over her shoulder and pouting while she listened to his answers.

David only grunted and shook his head.

Kora was growing used to David's grunts. That was the way he had answered most of Ty's questions today. Especially after the first fifty or so. 'She reminded me a little of my brother, Atym. I think they would be about the same age.'

'At least Atym is your brother,' he said. 'Ty is not my sister.' His eyes narrowed and he scowled darkly. 'She's not even my stepsister. She is nothing to me. And neither is Rodney.'

Kora watched the emotions flow over David's face. 'Why do you say that?' she asked. 'Do you not like Rodney?' With his kind face and strange eating habits,

Rodney had seemed harmless enough to her.

David just grunted again, and she thought that was all the answer she was going to get. Then he sighed and lifted his gaze to look at her. She could see he was angry and defensive, but there was also sadness in his eyes. 'He's okay, I suppose,' he said. 'But he's not my dad. Mum thinks I need a father-figure, but he's nothing like my father.'

She waited for him to continue, but he fell silent.

She leaned forward on her cushions. 'David? Earlier today, after we had walked to the shops together, you said you wanted to ask me something.'

He nodded. 'I did. I mean, I do.'

'Is it about your father?'

'Yes.'

He leaned back into the cushions. 'It's a long story, Kora.'

She shrugged. 'But not boring, I think.'

'Perhaps not,' he sighed. 'But it is sad.' He toyed with the broken watch on his wrist for a moment. 'He was a good father,' he said. 'The best. We did everything together.' He glanced up at her. 'You know, camping, fishing, hiking. We had an old motorbike we were fixing up together. It was going to be mine.'

She could see the pain in his eyes as he remembered. 'What happened to him?'

David's brow creased. 'War broke out. Dad was in the Army. He was a soldier.' He shrugged. 'He was sent off to fight in that stupid war.'

'Was he killed there?'

'No!' David's eyes blazed at her for a moment. Then he said more softly, 'No. No one really knows what happened to him. They were out on patrol in Afghanistan one day and he went missing.' He shook his head, disbelievingly. 'One minute he was there, patrolling with the rest of the men. And then the next minute he'd vanished. They searched the whole area for him but found nothing.' He sucked in a long breath. 'Apparently no shots were fired that day, and the Army is convinced that no prisoners were taken, either.'

Kora raised her eyebrows. 'And then?'

'Because no body was ever recovered he was listed as "missing in action, presumed dead".' His eyes flicked back up to Kora's face. 'But they can't be sure he's dead, Kora. Maybe he was taken prisoner, after all.'

Kora nodded. She could hear David's pain as he spoke about his father. His eyes dropped back to the broken watch he wore on his wrist. 'This is … was … my dad's watch, you know.'

'Did he give it to you before he disappeared?'

David nodded. 'He must have left it in my room for

me before he went away. But I didn't find it for months — long after he had gone to war.'

Kora looked at David's uncertain blue gaze. There was something more to the story, she thought. Something he wasn't telling her. His eyes held hers for a long moment. Finally he seemed to come to a decision, and he leaned forward intently, elbows propped on his knees.

'At least, that's what everyone else believes happened, Kora, but I don't think it's true.' He shook his head. 'The watch turned up mysteriously in my room on the day we were notified he was missing in action.'

'How did it get there, then?'

He shook his head. 'I don't know. But I'm sure I would have seen it. He'd been in Afghanistan for months!'

He lifted one shoulder in a half shrug. 'You know something else, Kora?' He fixed her with his steady blue gaze. 'Everyone thinks I'm imagining things, but I'm sure he was wearing this watch the day he left.' He exhaled heavily. 'And — it was working perfectly.'

Kora stared at David. He seemed so convinced. Could it be true? On Genesia, strange things like this happened all the time. But with humans? How could it be?

David was watching her face closely. 'Do you believe me?'

She thought for a moment before she spoke. Why

would he lie? Was it because he didn't want to believe his father was dead? She put her words together carefully. 'I think you believe that what you are saying is the truth, David,' she said. 'But I do not know yet whether it is or not.'

He nodded, subsiding back into the cushions against the wall.

'So that is what you wish, David?'

'What?'

'The question you wanted to ask me earlier. You wish for me to help you find your father.'

By royal command

The moment her eyes opened she knew she was alone. She could feel the absence of Amurru's energy. She swung her legs off her bed and called his name out anyway, knowing he would not answer and in the same moment knowing something was wrong.

The whisper of hushed voices reached her and she looked out over David's room. Amurru was sitting next to David on his bed. Both wore serious expressions and every now and then David would glance toward her globe. She used her magic to amplify their voices.

'If you care for her at all,' Amurru said, 'you will do as I have asked.'

The sense of something not being right gnawed away at her and she shimmered from her globe into the room. David jumped guiltily but Amurru simply nodded at her. 'Good morning, Empress.'

She crossed her arms. 'It will be when you tell me what

exactly is going on.'

Amurru's yellow eyes held hers and the expression in them filled her with dread. 'I was summoned during the night.' He paused. 'It is your brother, Empress.' Amurru bowed his head. 'He has been harnessed.'

Her stomach heaved and her legs wobbled. It felt like time stood still. Her brain was screaming that this could not be true, not Atym. Her eyes focused on Amurru.

'But how could they get inside the castle?' she choked out. 'A harnessed genie cannot get in.'

'Your father was not sure. But they think he was taken just outside the city walls.'

'But Atym is confined to the castle.'

Amurru looked sad. 'Your father thinks that Atym was somehow lured outside.'

'What could possibly tempt Atym to do that? And how could he do that without someone seeing?'

'Some genies passing by did think they saw something.' Amurru reached out his stumpy, withered hand to her. 'They thought they saw you.'

'Oh, Atym.' She dropped her face in her hands. 'How could he let himself be tricked so easily?'

'Your brother is only seven and he was missing you terribly.' Amurru sighed. 'The Emperor leaves this morning in search of him.'

'How does he intend to do that? To take enough soldiers with him to go up against Vennum would leave the castle without enough protection.'

'That is true,' said Amurru. 'That would leave the city most vulnerable.'

Her eyes flickered as suspicion dawned. 'You did not answer my question, Amurru. How many does he take?'

Amurru's gaze did not waver. 'He goes alone.'

Her power rumbled in her chest, yearning to burst out and summon the fiercest of hurricanes. How could her father do this? It was exactly what Vennum wanted. In fact, Vennum couldn't lose. Either her father would risk himself or he would risk the castle, because they all knew he would not abandon his son to Vennum. Not without a fight.

She turned to Amurru. 'I must go back.'

'And do what?' asked Amurru. 'Risk the destruction of the royal blood line?'

Her bangles jangled madly as she placed a hand on each hip. 'What is the point of a royal blood line if there is no empire to return to?'

Amurru slid off the bed and shuffled to her. 'Should Vennum succeed,' he reached out a small, stubby hand to her, 'then Genesia's only chance to live on lies in you.'

She shook his hand off. 'I will not stand back and

watch while Vennum destroys my family.'

Amurru glanced at David. 'Empress, you have no choice.'

'Please, David.' She placed her hand on his arm. 'Unharness me.'

'I am so sorry about your brother.' He gently removed her hand. 'But I will not unharness you.'

Understanding dawned as the small part of the conversation she had overheard came back to her. Amurru had asked David not to unharness her.

'Please, David. You more than anyone know how it feels to have a loved one taken from you. Would you not have given anything to go after your father? To find him and bring him back, no matter what the cost to you?'

David took a deep breath. 'Yes.' His eyes darted to Amurru. 'But it doesn't change anything.'

'You will not miss out, David.' Her eyes pleaded with him. 'I will grant all the wishes you can think of before you unharness me. In fact, I will even promise to return to you when my family is once again safe.'

He gave a violent shake of his head. 'I can't, Kora. I won't!'

'You can. Try to understand how important this is.'

'I do understand and I know how you feel.'

'Then free me. I can change things but I need to go now.'

'I've seen Vennum and all his harnessed genies. Are you really powerful enough against all of them?' His voice became louder, harder. 'And even if you are, what then? You told me yourself that a genie cannot harm a human.'

'Please, David. I beg you. I cannot do nothing.'

He stepped away from her. 'I'm sorry.'

Frustrated tears sprang to her eyes but she held them in. 'You stupid, selfish human, you have no idea what you are doing.' Then she spun on Amurru. 'Look what you have done. I shall never forgive you.'

'I have done my duty, Empress.' Amurru blinked his yellow eyes slowly at her. 'Your father's last command to me was to keep you safe here on Earth.'

She thought of her little brother, harnessed by Vennum, and her father leaving the castle all alone in search of him. What would he do? He must have a plan of some sort. Maybe he was even considering doing a deal with the Slaytians. Had it had come to that? Whatever his plan was, she knew he was unlikely to succeed alone. He needed help, her help! And yet here she was trapped on this stupid planet by a selfish, stupid human. She glared at Amurru, feeling betrayed. He had left her while she was asleep to manipulate David. She did not understand how Amurru could stand by and watch Vennum destroy their home.

'Does my father have a plan?' Kora asked, her voice quivering with rage. 'It is a mistake for him to go off on his own like that!'

'He did not say, Empress.'

'But he is alone, Amurru. Alone outside the city walls.' She threw her hands up in the air helplessly. 'He will have to travel on foot, without the use of his magic!' The very thought of this filled her with terror. What if her father was forced to use magic for some reason? Even the smallest trickle of power used out in the Genesian wilderness would lead Vennum straight to him.

'He will be careful, Empress,' said Amurru. 'He knows his enemy well.'

'He is so vulnerable, Amurru.' She knew Amurru was trying to reassure her, but she also knew the enormous risk her father was taking. 'How could I bear it if Father was also harnessed by Vennum?'

Amurru's eyes were full of sympathy. 'Your father has promised to be in touch for your birthday, and he said to tell you that he loves you very much.'

The tears she had held back stung her eyes again. She had not cried since she was a small child and she certainly wasn't about to do so now in front of Amurru and David. She turned her back on them. If they refused to help her then she would figure out a way to get home on her own.

Her birthday was still seven days away. She could not wait that long for news. She refused. She would help her family, and no stupid human or armourowl would be able to stop her!

For friends and fathers

Kora heard the front door of the house slam. She knew that David had only been waiting for his mother to leave for work so that he could summon her. At least that was one bonus of being kept a secret, he could only summon her when they had complete privacy.

She suspected that David wanted to talk. But that was only because he felt guilty about his refusal to unharness her. Her forehead creased into a scowl. And he should feel guilty. But what good would talking do? The only thing that would help her father now was action. She needed to do something. She had to come up with a plan.

'Kora?' David's voice floated into her globe. 'Please come out. I want to talk to you.'

She shook her head. Why should she go to him? She didn't feel like talking right now. She crossed her arms, staring at Amurru defiantly. But Amurru only blinked at her until finally she relented. If she didn't go, David would only wish it.

She shimmered into his room, an angry retort on her lips. But she swallowed her words when she saw him. He stood in the middle of the room, a silver tray in his hands. On it was a steaming cup of tea, a mound of chocolate chip cookies, and two crumpets dripping with melted butter and honey. A little vase on the tray held a couple of yellow daisies from the garden. Her anger drained away as she realised it was for her.

She stared up at his face. 'You made all this for me?'

'Who else?'

'But you went to so much trouble. You could have just wished for it, David.'

'I wanted to do it for you myself.' He shrugged as he put the tray down on the desk. 'It's not the same if you have to make it yourself. Even if you do use magic.'

She sat down on the edge of the bed and David passed her the tea. He propped himself against the edge of the desk, watching her. 'Go on, drink it,' he said. 'It'll make you feel better.'

She doubted that. It would take more than a cup of tea to make things better. But she lifted the cup and sipped. It was hot and sweet and milky. And David was right, it did calm her nerves a little. She looked up at him and smiled.

'Thank you.'

He shrugged. 'It's nothing.'

She didn't answer, but she was touched. No one had ever made her anything before. At least, not without using magic. She took another sip of her tea and waited for him to speak.

'Kora?'

'Mmm?'

'I really am sorry about Atym. And your father.' He stared down at his feet. 'But I just can't let you risk your life, too.'

'I know you mean well, David, but surely it is my decision to make.' Kora shook her head as she spoke. 'It is not for you to decide whether I risk my life. And it is not for Amurru to do so, either.'

'But if I did let you go,' said David, 'what good would it do? What could you do to help either of them?'

'I would think of something.'

David stood and strode across the room, agitated. 'You told me yourself that no genie can harm Vennum because he is half-human. You would only risk being harnessed by Vennum yourself. Surely that would only make things even worse for them?'

Kora shrugged. 'I do not know what I will do yet, David. But I will come up with a plan.' Her voice remained defiant but in her heart she knew he was right. There was so little she could do. 'He is my father, David. How can I sit by doing nothing when he is in grave danger? If I could just go back to Genesia, at least I would be there to comfort my mother. She waits alone in the palace not knowing whether any of her family is safe.'

'Can't you just open one of those viewing portals? Then you could see for yourself whether they are safe?'

She shook her head. 'I could never do that from here. It would take an incredible amount of power to open a portal on Genesia from Earth. Even if I was powerful enough, using so much magic would certainly attract Vennum's attention.'

'Okay, but what about your mother?' he asked. 'She could use one to keep an eye on your father? Or to see where Atym is?'

Again she shook her head. 'No, a viewing portal does not work that way. A portal can only be opened onto a specific location, not onto a specific genie or person. You remember the one I opened onto Panda Rock the other day, when we watched Vennum and his genies?'

'How could I forget?'

'I was able to open that one because I had been there. I had a fix on the exact location. Vennum could be on Earth right now and I would not know. I could only open a portal to view him if I knew his exact location.'

He nodded. 'I guess it's just as well it works that way, otherwise Vennum would have been able to find us using one.'

Kora stepped towards him, her mind swirling with ideas. 'Yesterday you asked me if I would help you find your father. What if I could help you find him?' Her voice was filled with hope. 'If I did, would you release me so that I could go and find mine?'

David stared at her. 'I don't need to bargain with you, Kora. I can just wish that you find my father.' He glanced away. 'I don't have to unharness you afterwards.'

Kora's mouth dropped open. 'You would do that? You would let me find your father for you, while you refuse to allow me to search for mine?'

She could see uncertainty flicker in David's eyes. But then his face hardened. 'You are trying to blackmail me,' he said. 'But it is an entirely different thing. No lives will be put at risk by searching for my father.'

She turned away from him, the intense disappointment making her shoulders slump.

'I can't believe you would do that to me,' he said. 'You would want me to live without my father, just because you can't be with yours?'

She stared out the window, thinking over his words.

Finally she turned back to face him. 'You are right, David,' she said. 'It is wrong of me to ask you to suffer just because I must. And you have suffered for five years. It is too long. Let us do it today. Right now.'

She tipped her head. 'Go ahead, David. Make your wish.'

The cave

'What do you mean you can't find him? I wished it.'
David mashed his hand through his messy hair. 'You have
to find him.'

She frowned in concentration. 'I am sorry, David.' She
placed the photo of David and his father down. 'He is not
here to be found.'

David dropped his head into his hands and took a few
deep breaths. When he lifted his head his gaze was steady
but sad. 'I wish,' he said, 'to go to my father's grave.'

She felt the agony behind his words. Her power
rumbled around in her chest seeking the answer to his
wish but something wasn't right. She could feel the pull
to a place, but she knew it was not his father's grave. She
increased her power and continued to search. 'David,' she
finally said, 'I cannot find him.'

'What do you mean? Why not? If you're supposed to
be such a powerful genie then why can't you find him?'

'If he was anywhere on this Earth I would have found him.' She swallowed her own frustration. Why could she not find him? 'It is as if he has vanished from the planet.'

David stared blankly at her. 'But how could that be? People don't just vanish into thin air. You must be doing something wrong. I thought you could find anybody anywhere?'

'I am not doing anything wrong. I should be able to locate any full-blooded human anywhere on the planet.'

'Then how come you can't find my father?'

'I cannot explain it, but there is something odd,' she said. 'I felt a kind of pull to a place.' She laid a hand gently on his shoulder. 'It is not your father's grave but I do feel it may be where your father died.'

She felt his shoulder shudder. 'I wish then,' he said, 'to go to the place my father died.'

The power that had been previously flowing directionless through her body gathered force and burst out, transporting them instantly.

She blinked in the harsh light. They were standing on scorching hot sand at the entrance to a cave in the middle of the most desolate place she had ever seen. The land was barren and endless.

She squinted up at David who was standing still,

looking shell-shocked. 'You think my father died here?' he asked.

'Yes,' she said. 'Inside the cave.'

She watched his shoulders rise and fall as he took a few deep breaths. Then he ducked his head and entered the cool darkness of the cave.

He stopped abruptly and touched a place on the cave wall, then crouched in front of it. The wall was darker here and she walked over to see what he was looking at.

'Is this my father's blood?'

She leaned in to examine the dark, red-black stain. 'Yes.'

David sank to his knees in the cool sand and bowed his head against the wall.

'But his body isn't here?' His voice was thick with emotion.

'No,' she answered hoarsely. 'I am so sorry, David.' She gently touched his arm and left him in the cave, his head leaning against the jagged wall. The hot, bright sunlight was a welcome relief from the icy fingers of death that seemed to lurk within the cave. With her own father now so vulnerable on Genesia, her heart ached in sympathy for David.

She summoned a cushion and a weather shield and sat down to wait. Her thoughts whirled around and around. She knew, without a doubt, that David's father had died in that cave, but where was his body? It really was as if he had vanished. If she could find out what had happened to David's father when he died, they may be able to find his grave.

It was believed that if a genie was powerful enough, that genie could open a viewing portal back into a past time. Few genies had ever been brave enough to try it and those that had, the stories went, had wound up dead, or nearly dead, from the exertion of using such an extreme amount of power. But just how powerful would you have to be? How much power would it require to open a portal through time and space, and how long could that portal be held open for?

She could taste the desire to try it. To be the first genie to ever achieve it, but now was not the time. That amount of power would draw Vennum immediately.

David's long shadow cast over her as he stepped out of the cave. His eyes were tinged with red, but his voice was even when he spoke. 'Thank you, Kora.'

'I am sorry we did not find your father.'

'At least I know now.' David plonked down on the cushion beside her. 'He's not ever coming home.'

Her heart twisted painfully imagining his grief. 'Is it better to know?' she asked. 'Or do you wish you could still hope?'

'I'm not sure.' He wiped the sweat from his brow. 'But I do know that everybody, living or dead, has the right to come home. He deserves to be laid to rest close to the people who loved him. Please, Kora. Is there any way, any way at all, for us to find his body?'

Two birds with one stone

Kora paced restlessly around her globe, deep in thought. 'You should try to stay calm, Empress,' Amurru said, his voice gentle. 'Your anxiety will not help the situation.'

'You may be happy to sit here waiting for my father to be harnessed.' She shook her head angrily. 'But I cannot! I must come up with a plan to help save him.' Her forehead creased in a deep scowl. 'And the rest of my family. All Genesia depends on it.'

They heard the front door of the house bang shut. David's mother had left for work. Through the viewing screens Kora saw David stride into the bedroom. In the next instant his voice rang out. 'I wish to come in and talk with you, Kora.'

She turned to watch David materialise in her home. He appeared next to Amurru's chair, shivering a little from the shock of transportation. 'I'm not sure I'll ever get used to that,' he said, glancing around the globe.

'Good morning, David,' said Amurru.

Kora didn't speak, but absently waved her hand towards the empty space next to David. A lounge chair appeared, covered in bright silk cushions. And a little round table with what she had come to know as David's favourite drink in the centre of it. An icy cold chocolate milkshake, with double malt.

'You've got dark rings under your eyes.'

Kora said nothing, but Amurru nodded. 'The Empress did not sleep well last night, David,' he said. 'As you know, many things worry her.'

'Has something else happened?' asked David.

Kora shook her head. 'We have no news of my father, if that is what you mean. But I know that is not what you came to talk to me about. You wish to know if I have thought any more on how we can discover what happened to your father's body?'

'I know this is not a good time for you,' replied David. 'But I have to know, Kora. I can't stop thinking about it.'

She let out a long, sad sigh. 'My thoughts have been heavily occupied trying to come up with a plan to help my own father.'

'But even if you could somehow get to Vennum without being harnessed, what could you do?'

'I know, I know. Genies cannot do anything to a

human, or even a filthy half-human like Vennum!'

'No,' said David, slowly. 'Genies can't hurt a human,' he turned to meet Amurru's knowing yellow gaze, and his voice rose excitedly, 'but another human can!'

Kora stared at him. 'What are you saying, David? That you would fight Vennum?' She flung one arm up into the air, bangles jangling loudly. The glow from the soft lamps reflected off the jewels spread across her fingers, sending colourful rainbows dancing across the ceiling of the globe. 'You have no idea what you would be up against.'

Amurru coughed wheezily. 'David makes a valid point, Empress.'

Her eyes flashed to Amurru. 'And that point is?'

'The point, Empress, is that perhaps the two problems are not mutually exclusive.'

David stared at Amurru. 'What do you mean?'

Amurru blinked slowly at him. 'There are two problems to be overcome. The first is how to discover your father's fate.'

'Yes.' David nodded. 'And the second problem is how to help Kora's father.'

Kora leapt to her feet and resumed her pacing. 'I see what you are getting at, Amurru.'

'What is he getting at?'

Amurru nodded, satisfied. He leaned back in his chair

to watch quietly, the hint of a tiny smile touching the edges of his eyes.

'We'll need a plan.' Kora's voice rose with excitement and hope. 'Something radical, that he could never suspect.'

'Who will never suspect?' asked David.

Kora began to pace faster as her mind whirled with ideas.

David was getting agitated. He leaned forward in his seat and his voice rose. 'Kora?' He turned to Amurru, but Amurru simply blinked at him.

Finally, David sprang to his feet. 'Will somebody please tell me what is going on?'

A window of hope

'Let me get this straight.' David stood between Kora and Amurru. 'You will find out what happened to my dad by some sort of time travel portal thing.'

'I will attempt,' interrupted Kora, 'to open a viewing portal back through time.'

'Right,' David nodded slowly. 'And that amount of power will bring Vennum and then you want me to kill him?'

A slow smile spread across Kora's face. 'If you kill him David, then so be it. But I would not ask that of you. All you have to do is make him unconscious.'

David blew out a long breath. 'And then what?'

'Rihando can take him to the Slaytians. They can use their mind power to direct his thoughts into unharnessing all the genies and then Rihando will be able to banish Vennum from Genesia.'

'And the Slaytians would do that?'

'For a price. But it does not matter now. With Atym harnessed my father will pay what they ask.'

'What about all the other genies that Vennum has harnessed?' David asked. 'Are they just going to stand around and watch while I knock Vennum out?'

Kora shook her head. 'No, they will not. Some of them are rebels who are on Vennum's side by choice and Vennum will have wished for the others to protect him.'

David pushed his hand through his long, messy hair. 'Should be a piece of cake then, huh?'

'You are right to be worried.' Amurru spoke quietly. 'This will not be easy.'

'And you are sure that a portal back through time is the only way of finding out what happened to my father?'

'Yes,' Kora nodded. 'But it has not been done successfully before.'

'But even just trying to do it will use enough power to draw Vennum?'

'Without a doubt!'

'How much time will we have before he comes?'

'Normally only a few seconds, but I have been thinking about that.' Kora began to pace her globe. 'If I can open the portal, then we may be able to actually step through it. If I close it after us then Vennum will not be able to see it or follow it, but he will be able to sense the use of power and be waiting for us when we get back.'

'What you suggest, Empress, is extremely dangerous. What if your power is so depleted that you cannot reopen the portal to get back?' Amurru wheezed. 'And even if you are successful you may not recover from such a drain on your power. You will certainly be weak and exhausted upon your return.'

Kora's dark eyes fixed on David. 'That's what the human is for. And we should, hopefully, have the element of surprise on our side.'

David took over pacing the globe. 'So if the portal works, and we don't get stuck back in time, then we will return to find Vennum waiting for us with his army of harnessed genies?'

'Yes.'

'And you will be exhausted and possibly of no help at all?'

'Yes.'

'And Vennum will want to kill me so he can harness you?'

'Yes.' She couldn't help but smile this time at the look on his face.

'And you are sure, really sure, there is no other way of finding out what happened to my dad?'

'No other way.'

David stopped pacing to stand directly in front of her. 'Then I guess we have a plan.'

With those few words the heavy weight around her heart began to lift a little. For the first time since she had been sent to Earth she felt she had reason to hope. It may be a long shot and they may not be successful, but at least she was finally going to be doing something. Something that had the chance to free Genesia of Vennum, and that was worth any risk. She thought she noticed a smug smile flit across Amurru's face but it was gone before he spoke.

'You must consider this carefully,' said Amurru. 'You will only get one chance at getting this right.'

David plonked back down on his chair. 'I guess you had better tell me everything you can about Vennum.'

'I can do better than that,' Kora grinned. She waved her hand and a screen appeared. 'I'll show you!'

Memories

Amurru shuffled over to sit down right next to David. 'A genie trick,' he explained. 'They can project a memory onto a screen.'

Kora smiled to herself at the look on David's face. Humans were easy to impress. She quieted her mind. It didn't take a lot of magic to do it but it did require concentration. Luckily, although she had been only seven at the time, it was one of the most vivid memories from her childhood. It was the day she had performed her first royal duty and seen her first real human. And the memorable day had ended dramatically with the birth of her baby brother.

Her heart sang as an image of her father appeared. He was looking at her with such love in his eyes.

'Is that your father, Kora?'

Her throat felt tight so she just nodded.

'It's strange,' said David. 'I can actually see he adores you.'

'You are seeing a memory,' explained Amurru. 'So you are seeing the emotions of that memory as well. Although you are also correct — the Emperor does adore her.'

Kora stared at her father on the screen. How well she remembered that day. It was the first time she had been out on official duty with her father, and she had been so proud. Her father was dressed in his formal red coat with the Genesian royal emblem embossed in gold on the front. Kora had also been wearing the royal emblem that day, embossed into the golden scarf that had held back her long, shiny hair.

It was a Genesian custom that every month her parents would travel together through the streets of the city on the royal flying carpet, waving to the people of Genesia, both to be seen and to see for themselves that all was well in their beloved city. This day her mother, who was heavily pregnant with Atym, had decided not to go, and her father had taken her along instead.

Kora sat on the front of the carpet, then snuggled back against her father's chest as they took off from the palace. It was an exhilarating way to travel.

Beside her David gasped as he watched the changing images on the screen. From the palace the carpet whizzed up and out over the rooftops. It was hard for her to imagine what it must be like for him, seeing Genesia for the first time. The glittering golden, domed rooftops glinting in the warm sunshine, and the immaculate paved streets below. The slim golden towers of the palace stretched far into the sky, reaching so high that puffy, white clouds were clustered around the tips. On the rooftop of the palace itself were stone figurines of tiny, winged demons that periodically sprang to life, travelling about the roof in fast little bursts shooting flaming arrows into the air.

Formidable stone walls surrounded the palace's extensive gardens, and sculptures of famous Genesians were carved into each pillar. At the entrance to the palace compound solid gold arches curved majestically over gleaming, polished wooden gates.

The blurring images on the screen slowed a little as the flying carpet soared down and along the city streets, just above the heads of the people. The roads were paved with red and yellow cobblestones, and filled with genies that shimmered in and out of view as they went about their business.

There were buildings lining the streets that drew the crowds, but unlike humans, Genesians had no need to shop. Most of the buildings were meeting places where genies gathered to socialise, eat and be entertained.

They had only zoomed down a few streets when

a deafening alarm blared from the screen and genies appeared and disappeared in coloured mist like firecrackers.

'The city alarm goes off when there is trouble at the gates,' said Amurru. 'The Empress is showing you the first time we met Vennum.'

The image on the screen shimmered and dissolved, and in that moment they were no longer hovering in the bustling city streets. 'We shimmered instantly to the city gates when the alarm sounded,' said Kora.

Stretching away on either side into the distance were the towering, solid silver walls that protected the city. Kora glanced at David. 'That wall you can see surrounds the entire city, and is the edge of the Genesian Protection Zone. There is only one set of gates into the city, and this is it.' She waved her hand at the imposing barred gates that stood closed in front of them, preventing the small family on the other side from entering the city. 'What you can see beyond those gates is the beginning of the Genesian wilderness.'

A cleared, barren strip of land stretched for several kilometres on the other side of the gates, beyond which the edge of the forest could be seen. Thick, black clouds were gathering in the sky and lay heavily over the forest. They spread darkly from the horizon to the city's edge where they banked up as if against an invisible barrier. In spite of the storm brewing all around, the vast circle of sky above the city remained a stunning azure blue, and the people in the streets below basked in the warm, golden sunshine.

Hundreds of guards in bright red coats stood in front of the city's barred gates. David pointed at the family standing outside the gates. 'Who are they?'

A teenage boy stood close by a tall, dark-haired man. An unconscious woman lay in the man's arms.

'The boy is Vennum. He is with his human mother, and his Genesian father, Scarvenn.'

Scarvenn dropped to one knee in front of the Emperor. 'I beg of you, Emperor, to give permission for the Slaytians to save my dying wife. Their forest medicines are my last and only hope.'

The Emperor's face looked like it was carved from stone. 'Already you have been banished from Genesia, and now you dare not only to return, but to also bring a human here. Both are crimes punishable by death.'

'I have already suffered so much, and my family is all I have left.' Scarvenn glanced at his son. 'We cannot live without her.'

'Her death is inevitable.' The Emperor's voice was grave. 'All human lives are short.'

'If our friendship ever meant anything to you,' implored Scarvenn, 'then you would make this one exception.'

The Emperor stood taller. 'You dare to speak to me of friendship after you tried to trick the Imperial Empress into marrying you?'

'Scarvenn wanted to marry Kora's mother many years ago,' whispered Amurru. 'If he had succeeded he would be the Emperor of Genesia now.'

David frowned. 'So Kora's mother is the Empress by birthright? '

The memories paused on the screen. 'She is,' said Kora. 'That is why she is called the Imperial Empress. But under Genesian law, once married both the husband and wife rule equally.'

Kora resumed the memory viewing.

Kora's heavily pregnant mother stepped into view and everyone looked towards her.

'Imperial Empress,' said Scarvenn. 'You have shown me great mercy in the past. I beg this one last request.'

Kora's mother hesitated, her wild hair shimmering around her as she contemplated the scene in front of her. And then the woman in Scarvenn's arms coughed. Blood trickled out of the corner of her mouth and her eyes fluttered open. She reached out a grasping hand for Vennum and he went to his mother, a terrified son watching his mother die. She looked weakly from Vennum to his father. 'I love you both,' she coughed again. 'So much.' She drew a last rasping breath and then fell limply back. The gold bands around Scarvenn's wrists and ankles that harnessed him to his human wife vanished. She was dead.

'She was the first human I had ever seen,' said Kora quietly. 'And then, still so young, she just died.'

The image on the screen continued. Vennum and his father were both looking down at the dead woman and then Scarvenn lifted his head and David shuddered. Tears streaked Scarvenn's face, but there was a torturous blaze in his eyes that was fearsome. 'You have taken from me, denied me, everything I have ever wanted.' Slowly, purposefully, he looked at the Imperial Empress and then his eyes fell and lingered on Kora. 'It will be your turn now, Emperor, to know loss and grief.'

Vennum glared resentfully through the gates and reached for his father. He put his arms around him and they both fell back in pain and shock.

Vennum clutched at the blistering purple burn on his arm and his father once again had glowing bands at his wrists and ankles. Everybody was dumbfounded, and then Vennum and his parents simply vanished.

'A half-human, half-genie cannot harness,' spoke Rihando, in disbelief.

'Well, this one can.' The Emperor raked a hand across his face. 'Take an army, Rihando.' The Emperor hesitated for a moment, and looked at his wife and then at Kora. 'Kill Scarvenn for his treason and banish his half-blood child from Genesia.'

Rihando bowed his head to his Emperor and then he, too, vanished.

The screen went blank and with a wave of Kora's hand it disappeared.

'So what happened to Scarvenn?' asked David. 'Was he killed?'

'We do not know. No one has ever reported killing him but he has never been seen again, either.' She shrugged. 'I guess he either died or Vennum wished him unharnessed.'

'And now Vennum wants the revenge that his father promised,' said David.

'It is more than a want.' Amurru spoke quietly. 'It has become his life's obsession to watch all of Genesia suffer the way that he has.'

'He was just a kid,' said David. 'Not much older than us, and now … he is a madman.'

Kora stiffened. 'He is insane,' she said. 'And he

becomes more evil with every passing day.'

'Watching that memory of you with your father, I can see how much he loves you.' David sighed. 'And yet he sent you here to Earth.'

'I know that my parents and the High Council were just trying to protect me, but I would have given anything to stay at home on Genesia.'

'It is not all bad, Empress,' wheezed Amurru. 'And you would have had to come to Earth in two years' time anyway for your Earth duty.'

David rubbed a hand across his chin. 'I don't suppose any genie ever wants to come to Earth.'

'No, not the royal genies and certainly not the banished ones.'

'So all royal genies are sent to Earth?'

'The High Council of Genesia usually sends us in our sixteenth year. They believe that we must first learn how to serve to learn how to rule.' She sighed. 'It is a lesson they like to see learnt young and learnt well.'

'What about the other genies that are banished here?'

'They are our worst criminals, who have been sentenced to death,' said Kora, 'but if the Emperor intervenes to grant them mercy, they can instead be banished to Earth for the remainder of their lives. That is the reason so many genies are described as mean and evil in your old stories and legends.' She shrugged. 'They are criminals.'

'So Scarvenn was a criminal?'

'Yes. He went to the Slaytians to ask them to use their mind power to influence my mother. It is a most serious crime to negotiate with a Slaytian without royal approval, but to be caught attempting to have a Slaytian influence the thoughts of an Imperial Empress, that is treason.'

David let out a long breath. 'Sounds like Vennum's father was power hungry.'

Kora nodded. 'And when he brought his human wife to the Genesian gates he broke a second law. No genie is allowed to bring a human to Genesia.'

David rubbed the burn on his arm. 'I feel sorry for any poor human that harnesses an evil genie.'

'Understand, David,' said Amurru, 'that you always have your own free will. And that just as evil thoughts lead to evil deeds, noble thoughts lead to noble deeds.'

'Or in Vennum's case,' said Kora, 'vengeful thoughts lead to vengeful deeds.'

'Let us hope, then, that he does not manage to harness you, Empress.' Amurru's round eyes blinked slowly at them. 'Or Vennum will indeed get his revenge and Genesia as we know it … will be gone.'

Dropping a bombshell

'Why is Marcia taking so long to leave for work this morning,' Kora snarled. Rodney always left home at first light, but Marcia didn't start work until 9.00 am.

Amurru sat quietly in his chair. 'David's mother is not leaving any later than usual, Empress,' he croaked. 'It is only your impatience that makes it seem so.'

'But we have much to do today, Amurru. And I have had an idea that I need to discuss with both you and David. That is, if his mother ever leaves us alone.'

Amurru smiled at her, about to reply. But then he stopped to listen, hearing something that Kora could not. His ears twitched and swivelled toward the bedroom door.

She waited, listening for a moment, until she could hear what Amurru's sharp ears had already picked up. David's mother was heading down the passage to his bedroom. That was unusual. Normally she simply called out a quick goodbye as she raced out the front door in a flap.

Kora and Amurru turned to look out of the globe. David sat on his bed, listening to his iPod. He seemed relaxed but Kora could tell that he was just as eager for his mother to leave as she was. His brow was furrowed and the fingers of one hand drummed restlessly against his knee.

He glanced up in surprise when his mother appeared in the doorway. He yanked the earphones out of his ears. 'Mum. What's up?'

'I'm just heading off to work.' She smiled uncertainly at him.

Kora laughed. 'I wonder what bombshell she is going to drop this time!'

Amurru barked out his strange, coughing laugh and nodded. 'Something that will not please David, it seems.'

David waited for his mother to continue. 'There's something I wanted to discuss with you before I go.'

'Okay,' he replied, his voice wary.

Marcia wrung her hands together nervously then blurted out her news. 'Tyra will be coming to stay with us for the rest of the summer holidays.'

David sprang to his feet to object, but Marcia put her hands up to silence him. 'I know what you're going to say, David, but Tyra is Rodney's daughter and as such is welcome here anytime.'

'But why, Mum?' He shook his head in disbelief. 'She lives with her mother!'

'Tyra's grandmother is very ill. Her mother has to travel to Europe for a couple of months to care for her.'

'Where will she sleep?' His face was suspicious now.

'Well, that's what I wanted to talk to you about,' said Marcia. 'Your room is the only one in the house suitable for someone Tyra's age.' She nodded her head vigorously as she spoke, as if willing him to agree. 'You can move to the sleep-out.'

'The sleep-out?' A look of horror spread over David's face. 'We don't have a sleep-out,' he yelled. 'That's a verandah!'

Marcia's face became stern. 'It's an enclosed verandah, David. It will be fine for you to sleep in for a couple of months. It's summertime. The nights are more than warm enough.'

'But Mum, this is my room. Why can't Ty sleep in the sleep-out?'

'Rodney and I talked last night and we feel it is best if Tyra sleeps in this room.'

He glared at his mother through his heavy fringe. 'And who's going to look after her while you and Rodney are at work?'

His mother didn't need to reply, it was obvious. David was the only person at home during the day. 'When is she moving in?'

'Tonight. Her mother has to leave immediately. You'll need to move all your things into the sleep-out today.'

'Today!'

'You will do it today, David,' she ordered. 'Make sure this room is empty and clean before I get home from work.'

David stared at her, speechless.

'Tyra has enough to deal with,' said his mother. 'The least we can do is to make her feel welcome. Especially over Christmas.' She turned to leave. 'And David, get your hair cut!'

He lifted one shoulder in a half shrug.

'That's an order.' She stared at his rebellious expression for a long moment. 'If you don't get it cut today,' she continued, her voice soft but dangerous, 'I'll cut it myself.'

Kora waited until she heard the front door bang shut, then shimmered down into David's room. Amurru appeared beside her a moment later.

David stared at them, his eyes sullen and angry.

'I am sorry, David.' She took a step towards him. 'But forget about your mother for the moment.' Her voice sped up in her eagerness to talk about their plans. 'I have something much more important to discuss with you and Amurru.'

His thunderous expression lifted a little. 'What is it?'

'I have been up all night, thinking,' she replied. 'And I have realised a few crucial things. The first is that we will need a safe place to time-travel from.'

'Of course,' he agreed. 'We can't open the viewing portal from here. That would only bring Vennum and his genies to our house.'

'Yes. It needs to be as far from here as possible.'

Amurru nodded. 'And it must be uninhabited.'

'Of course,' said Kora. 'There must be absolutely no chance of there being any people for miles around.' Her eyes shone with the strange mixture of fear, excitement and hope. 'We do not want any innocent people killed just for being in the wrong place at the wrong time.'

David's eyes lit up. 'Get me an atlas, Kora. I think I know the perfect place.'

Complications

The last five days had been the most frustrating of Kora's life. Ty the Spy was forever snooping about. With Marcia and Rodney at work all day it meant the only person around for her to snoop on was David, and she was relentless. It felt like she had touched every item in David's sleep-out, including her globe, despite the fact that it was still camouflaged as a rock.

Her main spy tool was an electronic password journal. If she found anything of interest, or if anyone, mainly David, did anything she thought they shouldn't, she would whip out her journal and write it down for future reference. One night Kora had taken a peek while Ty slept, just to make sure she hadn't discovered anything that might expose her. The journal said things like, *Thursday, 10.04 am, heard a girl's voice coming from David's room. Friday, 12.52 pm, David used a swearword.*

David's new room offered almost no privacy, so

between Ty hanging about all day and everyone either walking through or looking out to the verandah, Kora and David were struggling to discuss their plans. Especially now they knew that Ty was eavesdropping on them and had already heard Kora's voice at least once.

Kora could hear raised voices again at the dinner table and knew it would only be a few more minutes until David would, like most other evenings, fling the verandah flyscreen door open and throw himself on his bed. She could hear David's mother going on again about his hair. She honestly couldn't fathom what all the fuss was about. She rather liked the way his long, messy hair fell across his face.

The raised voices grew even louder, and Kora opened a viewing portal to see what was going on.

'I didn't feed it to Cuddles,' yelled David. 'It just fell onto the floor.'

Ty slammed her voice recorder down next to her plate. 'You did so. You always do and it makes him puke.'

'You're such a dobber, Ty. And after I took the blame for you eating the whole packet of chocolate biscuits yesterday.'

Rodney's face turned bright red. 'Is that true, Ty? Did you lie to me?'

Ty screwed her face up in anger. 'So what? David lies

all the time.' She poked her finger at him. 'He had a girl in his room, and he's supposed to be grounded.'

'I did not,' said David. 'And you're the liar, not me.'

Ty gasped, and reached out to press a button on her voice recorder. The table fell silent as Kora's lilting, accented voice filled the air.

David lurched from his seat and grabbed Ty's recorder, flinging it against the kitchen wall, where it shattered and dropped to the floor in a million pieces. He stormed from the kitchen to the sound of Ty's wailing.

The crash of the flyscreen opening hard enough to hit the wall heralded David's return to the sleep-out. Marcia's angry voice followed. 'Don't think there won't be any consequences for this behaviour, David!' she yelled.

Kora didn't dare go out to talk to him, it was too dangerous with everyone in the house and the verandah so open. They had agreed for her to wake him about 1.00 am so they could sneak out and finish making their plans. The middle of the night was the only time they could talk properly now. Usually they just went far enough away to not disturb the house, although one night they had taken a midnight trip to the desert in the middle of Australia — to the place David had determined that they should time-travel from.

She stretched out on her bed to wait. It seemed that

wait was all she did these days. But maybe the waiting was nearly over. Tonight they would finalise their plans and tomorrow was her birthday and her father had promised to check in with her. She hoped it was a promise he would be able to keep, and she would finally have some news from home. How her heart ached for her family.

Time ticked away and she could hear that David had finally fallen asleep. Although her own thoughts began to drift she knew she would never be able to sleep with all the plans running through her head. The creak of the floorboards told her that Marcia was checking on her son, peering through the door like she did every night, before going to bed herself. She rolled over to look out of her globe and was surprised to see Marcia quietly push the door open and come into the room. This was unusual and Kora watched her lean over her son. She saw the glint of something metal in the moonlight as Marcia bent closer to David.

Kora bolted upright. Marcia was grabbing the long, messy strands of David's hair and jaggedly lopping them off with a pair of scissors.

David's arm knocked her away as he jerked awake. 'What are you doing?'

Marcia dropped the cut-off hair onto David's bed. Her voice was tight when she spoke. 'I warned you if you didn't cut it that I would do it myself.'

David bolted out of bed and flicked on the light. Large chunks of his hair were missing, and his fringe had been reduced to spiky, uneven little tufts.

David reached up to touch his hair. 'I can't believe you did that!'

Marcia looked as horrified as her son but simply turned on her heel and left without another word.

Kora shimmered into the room. At first David didn't acknowledge her, but then with a face carved from stone he turned to her.

'I wish,' he said, 'for an electric clipper.'

With a heavy heart she waved her hand and did as he requested. Without a word he plugged it in and began shearing off his hair. It was fast and thorough and within a couple of minutes the floor was covered in soft clumps of his hair.

When he was done he turned to face her and handed her back the clippers. 'It's just hair, Kora. No big deal.' He tried to smile but it didn't reach his eyes. 'At least when we go to war I'll look like a soldier.'

She wasn't sure what to say to him so she waved her hand and the clippers and all the hair on the ground disappeared. It was so strange to think that a week ago she would have found the sight of Marcia chopping away at

David's hair hilariously funny, yet now it just made her sad. It was amazing how much things could change in such a short time.

David flopped into a chair. 'What time is it?'

'Just after midnight.'

He leaned down and pulled out a huge parcel from under the bed. 'Guess that means it's okay to give you this, then.' With a shy smile he handed her the parcel. 'Happy birthday.'

She felt surprised and strangely happy that he had thought to get her a gift. When had he even had the chance to go shopping?

'I had to bribe Ty to pick it up for me,' he said, as if reading her mind. 'Three hours of Cluedo before she agreed.'

Kora took a deep breath before slowly unwrapping the parcel. Inside was a giant panda bear. 'Oh, David, thank you. I love it!'

'I know you could just magic one up but I wanted to get you one the human way.'

She hugged the soft panda to her. It reached from her head to her knees. 'It is perfect.'

His face looked pleased and embarrassed at the same time. 'How long until we can get going?' he asked, changing the subject.

She opened a portal on Ty's room. She was snuggled up in bed, her narrow face relaxed in sleep and her journal tucked securely under one arm like a teddy bear.

She then opened a portal on Marcia and Rodney. They were both awake. Marcia looked like she had been crying and Rodney was gently holding her. Then, while they watched, Rodney began to kiss her. David made a disgusted noise and she quickly closed the portal. 'I guess we should wait a little longer,' she said.

David was running an agitated hand over his short, prickly hair. 'Nah, stuff it,' he said. 'Let's go now!'

Party planning

Kora leaned back against the oversized cushions on the ground, her legs stretched out before her on a thick, woollen blanket. She gazed up at Panda Rock. The moon was only a thin sliver in the inky, black sky, but it was surrounded by a sea of glittering stars and there was just enough light to be able to make out the shape of the panda's smiling face. David settled down against his own cushions beside her, still licking the icing from her pink, gooey birthday cake off his fingers.

In spite of everything that she'd had to deal with lately — the worry about her father and brother, the looming confrontation with Vennum, and all the waiting and planning she had done over the past week — a contented smile found its way onto her face. She hadn't expected to enjoy her fourteenth birthday much, but David's gift and then the enormous midnight birthday feast he had wished for when they arrived at their little clearing in the forest had warmed her heart.

Beside her, David burped loudly. 'That was good food, Kora,' he said, rubbing contentedly at his stomach. 'Where did you learn to cook like that?'

She grinned. 'Cooking looks much too complicated for me. But all food tastes good when you are hungry.'

He nodded and Kora laughed. David was always hungry, it seemed. Although it wasn't really surprising — ever since Rodney had moved in and taken over the cooking, there had been nothing but slimy lentils and spinach for dinner.

She drew in a long breath. The air was cooler now this late at night, but still heavy and fragrant. She listened to the myriad sounds coming from the forest, enjoying the soft sighing of the wind through the trees and the rustling of small creatures fossicking amongst the leaves on the forest floor. She especially liked the strange hooting calls of the night birds. But there was much to be discussed and they had to get back before Ty the Spy woke. The previous morning she had poked her head into David's sleep-out at just after 5.00 am!

Finally Kora sighed and pushed herself upright so she could sit cross-legged on the blanket. 'I guess we should finalise our plan,' she said. 'We'll need to get back soon.'

'We've nutted out most of it,' he said. 'We just need to

iron out some of the smaller details.'

Her brow furrowed in concentration. 'I was thinking that we should go at night.'

'Good idea,' he replied. 'That will make it harder for Vennum to see what we're doing.'

'And your family will be less likely to notice your absence,' she added.

He nodded and Kora continued. 'Then we wait there for at least half an hour, to make sure any trace of our magic trail has disappeared.'

'And you're certain that will be long enough to ensure Vennum and his genies can't follow our trail back home to Panda Rock?'

'Yes, David. I am certain.' She gave him a small smile. 'No magic trail could last longer than that.' She reached out her hand to touch his arm. 'I would not knowingly put your family in danger.'

He lifted his hand to shove at his long fringe, looking surprised when he found nothing but short stubble on top of his head. 'And while we are waiting for the magic trail to disappear we can make sure we have everything we need for our attack on Vennum.'

'Yes,' she replied.

'Then when we're ready you'll open the portal that will take us back in time.'

She nodded. 'That is what I hope. I guess we will just have to wait and see if I am powerful enough to do it.'

'How long do you think it will take Vennum to arrive?'

'About five seconds, maybe even less. However long it takes his genies to alert him to the use of such a colossal amount of power.' She lifted one shoulder in a half shrug. 'Then Vennum and his entire army will be there, ready to fight.' She thought of the battle that lay ahead of them. 'And I will be too weak to help you.'

'But as long as we can get through the portal in those few seconds before he arrives, he won't be able to see us?'

Kora nodded. 'But there are a lot of ifs in the plan. If I can open a large enough portal, if I can take the portal back to the right point in time, if I have any strength left to move after opening it, if we can get through it and if we close it behind us in the few seconds we have before Vennum arrives.'

He gripped both her hands in his, making her bangles jingle. 'Kora, I have every faith in you. Let's agree to make our plans assuming that you will be able to do it.'

David paused and leaned in closer to her. 'When you say we will actually be back in time, what exactly do you mean? That we will be there for real? In person?'

'I believe so.' Kora pursed her lips. 'We should really

be there, just as if we belonged in that time.'

He whistled softly, shaking his head in amazement.

She tried to meet his gaze but his eyes were glassy and unfocused. 'David?'

His brow was creased in thought. 'So what you're saying, Kora, is that I might actually be able to see my father again in person? For real?'

So that was it! Kora sighed. 'It may be possible. But I cannot say for sure.'

He leaned back from her, his expression unreadable. 'I could see my father again,' he repeated, his voice so low she could barely hear it. 'I could say goodbye.'

'Maybe,' she replied. 'But even if we can do it, he will be confused about who you are and how you got there. You are so much older now and we do not know what will be happening to him at the time.'

He nodded, but she could tell he wasn't really listening. She glanced up at the sky. It was still dark, but a soft pink light glowed against the horizon and it wouldn't be long before it was light.

She closed her eyes. It was probably only half an hour or so until the sun rose on her fourteenth birthday. She thought of her father's promise to contact her on her birthday and wondered if Amurru had been summoned to Genesia yet.

She pushed herself to her feet. Suddenly she was very keen to get back to her globe. She grabbed David's hand and hauled him up. With one wave of her fingers all their blankets and cushions vanished.

'Ready?' She barely waited for his nod before they shimmered, not into David's little sleep-out bedroom on the verandah, but directly into her globe.

Distractions

Kora and David stared through the viewing portal. The kitchen light was on. Marcia's tear-stained face looked tired as she sipped a cup of chamomile tea. Rodney paced the kitchen, stopping every now and then to peer out the kitchen window into the pre-dawn light.

'Your mother came to the room about ten minutes after you left.' Amurru pointed a stumpy finger at David. 'When she found you gone she thought you had run away.'

David grazed a hand through the stubble on his head. 'It's not like the thought hasn't crossed my mind.'

Amurru sighed. 'Rodney convinced her not to call the police. He said you would be coming back because you had not taken any of your belongings with you.'

'They went through my stuff!'

'Your mother was distraught that you were missing.'

The word 'missing' seemed to hang in the air. A

word that was painful for all of them. Kora glanced sympathetically at David. 'Would you like me to shimmer you outside so you can come in through the front door?'

David was very still. They watched as Rodney paced over to Marcia and squeezed her shoulder before dropping a kiss on her head.

'No,' said David. 'Let her stew a little longer.'

Amurru abruptly turned and shuffled away from them. 'I have been summoned,' he said, flexing his long, amber wings.

Kora sighed with relief. 'I thought the waiting would never be over.'

Amurru simply nodded and silence fell between Kora and David. Finally David turned his back on the scene in the kitchen. His eyes flicked to Amurru, cocooned inside his wings. 'Looks like you'll have some news soon.'

'Let us hope it is good news at last.'

An awkward silence stretched out between them as they waited.

'Distract me,' he said.

'What do you want me to do?' She pulled a face. 'Cartwheels?'

A tiny smile tugged at his bottom lip. 'You know, I really would have thought having a genie would be better than this.'

She shrugged. 'I did warn you.'

'How would you have celebrated your birthday if you were at home?'

She knew he was only trying to take his mind off his own family problems so she answered him. 'There would have been a grand feast in my honour, followed by the Tournament of Terrible Talents.'

'What's that?' asked David.

'It is the funniest game. Genies compete in a series of four difficult tasks. There is only one rule — they must complete the tasks without using any magic.' Kora grinned. 'Just like humans.'

David laughed. 'I guess that would be difficult for a genie.' He looked thoughtfully at her. 'I forget sometimes you have a whole other life there waiting for you. I suppose you have a best friend, too?'

'Yes, her name is Bonnetta. We have been close friends since we were babies.' Kora smiled. 'She is very sweet and I am always in trouble for leading her into mischief.'

David grinned. 'I can imagine that!'

'She is not particularly powerful but she is incredibly beautiful. She has many admirers.'

'I never thought to ask you that, Kora.' David frowned. 'Do you have an admirer?'

She sighed. 'It would not matter if I had a thousand.

My fate is already decided.'

'What do you mean?'

'I am to marry a Clawdonian genie.'

'Marry!' The word choked out of him.

'His name is Talon.'

'How long have the two of you been together?' His question sounded more like an accusation.

'We are not.' She half smiled at the shock on David's face. 'Not together, that is. I have only met him once. He lives on another planet.'

'Then why would you marry him?'

'Relations between Genesia and Clawdonia have long been rather strained. My parents and the High Council believe our marriage would unite the two.'

'But what about you? Don't you get a say?'

'I am an empress,' she shrugged. 'Duty comes first.'

'Don't you care that you'll have to spend the rest of your very long life with someone you don't love?'

She did not want to think about marriage to Talon and she certainly did not want to talk about it with David. 'It is complicated,' she said, with no attempt to hide her irritation.

'Okay, then. New topic. Why don't we go over how we will attack Vennum when we come back through the portal?'

'All right,' she said, thankful for the change of subject. 'I will make us gasmasks.'

'And we'll put them on before we come back through the portal?' asked David.

'Yes.' Kora looked steadily at him. 'The moment, the very second, we are back you will need to be ready to release the chloroform bomb. Otherwise they may have time to wish for their own masks.'

David nodded. 'Why don't we just come back ten minutes earlier, then?'

'We cannot,' replied Kora. 'That would mean we would actually see ourselves opening the portal to leave.'

'And that's a problem?'

'It is believed that if you see another version of yourself when you time-travel, one version of you will die.'

David looked shocked. 'How can you be sure we won't see ourselves?'

'I will take a fix on the exact moment we leave, and will attempt to return to it.'

'Don't worry, I'll be ready,' said David. 'Are you sure the chloroform bomb will be big enough to take out all the genies?'

'It will not only knock them out but it will keep them unconscious for at least ten minutes.'

'Then you'll put a mask on Rihando to wake him up?'

'I will, but I will also make a spare for you to carry in a backpack.' She looked into his worried eyes. 'If I am too weak you will need to place the mask on Rihando.'

'You will recover, though, won't you?' asked David. 'You'll only be exhausted for a bit?'

'The truth is, I do not know for sure. Sometimes if a genie's magic is depleted enough they do not recover, and even if they do recover, they may not be the same as they were before.'

'Are you sure you want to do this?'

'I am sure,' she nodded. 'What other choice do we have?'

'And you trust Rihando to take Vennum to the Slaytians?'

'I would trust Rihando with my life. He will know what to do.'

'And the Slaytians?'

'They are not so trustworthy. But I do believe they will do what we ask. There is too much they want.'

Amurru uncurled his wings and settled them back into place against his silver suit. Kora and David turned immediately. His look of grave concern had them both stepping toward him. Something was seriously wrong.

'What is it?' Kora's voice broke as she spoke. 'What has happened?'

Amurru shuffled near enough to take her slender hand in his stumpy grip. 'I am so sorry to have to tell you this.' He took a slow, wheezy breath. 'It is your father, Empress. He is missing.'

The point of no return

Kora was frantic. Her magic rumbled in her chest, barely under control. 'Please, Empress,' Amurru croaked. 'We must remain calm.'

'Um, Amurru?' David's voice was tentative. 'Exactly how do we know Kora's father is missing?' His eyes flickered from Amurru's face to Kora's, and back again. 'I mean, wasn't he supposed to be out in the wilderness, alone, without magic?' He shrugged. 'I thought no one was supposed to know where he was.'

'That is true, David.' Amurru nodded. 'But it has now been confirmed that the Emperor had planned to journey to the Slaytians. Along the way he was to rest at Tarru's house. Tarru is my nephew and lives deep in the wilderness.'

Kora gasped. 'So you did know where he was going!'

'To help ensure the safety of the Emperor his exact journey plan was kept a close secret by the High Council.'

Amurru let out a long, wheezy sigh. 'Even I did not know his planned destination until now.'

'But I still don't get it.' David's brow furrowed in confusion. 'How can they be sure he is missing? Maybe he's still on his way there.'

Amurru blinked his yellow eyes at David. 'If that is the case, then his journey is taking far longer than anticipated.' Amurru glanced anxiously at Kora before continuing. 'The Emperor was to have arrived there several days ago. He planned to rest there until today, Kora's birthday.'

'So that is how he was going to contact me for my birthday.' Kora let out a long, weary breath. 'He would have planned for Tarru to teleport himself to the High Council, delivering my father's report along with his birthday message for me.' Her voice hitched as she spoke.

Amurru nodded. 'The Council received word from Tarru late yesterday.' He shook his head. 'Words cannot express my sorrow at having to be the bearer of this dismal news, Empress.' His shoulders slumped as he looked at her stricken face. 'Tarru has searched, but there has been no sign of your father since he left the palace a week ago.'

They all fell silent. A long moment passed as they absorbed the news that Kora's father was officially missing.

Kora did not want to say it aloud, but she knew it

was likely that her father had been harnessed by Vennum. Despair twisted in her chest. She tried to block out the images that were flooding her thoughts. The horror of her father and brother in Vennum's power, having to obey his every whim. She knew her father would be distraught at being forced to turn against his own people. She had expected to fight Vennum but she had never imagined she might have to fight her own father and brother!

'I'm so sorry, Kora,' said David, his voice barely a whisper. She knew he understood the helplessness she felt.

She nodded at him. But she couldn't give up now. There was no way she was going to let Vennum win. She was Kora Archein, Empress of Genesia. She would do everything within her power to save Genesia and her family. She at least had to try!

'We have to do it now, Amurru. And there is not a moment to lose.'

She grabbed David's hand. 'Come on,' she said. 'We are as ready as we are ever going to be.'

'You mean we should leave now?' asked David. 'But it's almost morning. I thought we were going to leave at night?'

She nodded. 'I cannot leave my father and Atym in Vennum's clutches for another moment.'

Fear flickered in David's blue eyes, but he just nodded. 'Okay, Kora.'

Amurru stood and walked across to them. He waved his hand at the portal where Marcia and Rodney still sat in the kitchen. 'What about your mother, David?'

David touched his hand to his shaven head and Kora saw the flash of anger cross his face. 'No,' he said. 'She can wait until we return.'

Amurru studied David's face for a long moment. 'You must realise, David,' he said, 'that there is a very real possibility you will not return.'

Kora took David's hand. 'Amurru is right, David.' She managed a small smile. 'Go and make peace with your family before we leave.'

David sighed and turned to gaze at his mother and Rodney through the portal.

Kora turned to watch them, too. She squeezed his hand. 'It might be the last chance you get.'

Moment of truth

She focused on the present. It took all her control to not let her thoughts wander to what-ifs or maybes. There was no room now for doubts, only the job at hand and that was to defeat Vennum.

She concentrated on the list she had made, carefully summoning each item. She looked up as David returned.

She could hear Marcia crying in the next room. 'Did you not make peace?' she whispered.

'Not really.' David rubbed tiredly at the stubble on his head. 'She asked me to never disappear like that again.'

'And what did you say?'

'The truth.' David turned to stare out the window. 'What I could tell her of it, anyway.'

'What exactly do you mean?'

'I told her I would be going away for a while and that I wasn't sure when I would be back, but that it was really important and something that I had to do.'

Kora was incredulous. 'What did she say to that?'

David sighed. 'She begged me not to leave and told me time and again how much I was breaking her heart.'

'Would it have been easier not to tell her?'

'Easier, yes.' He turned away from the window. 'But it would hurt her more to simply find me missing again.'

Kora looked sympathetically at him. The human boy in front of her was so much more than she had expected when she had first met him. She handed him the backpack she had prepared. 'The spare mask and the chloroform bomb are in there, plus a couple of other emergency items.'

He opened it and had a look through the contents. Then he zipped it up and swung it easily onto his back. 'And our masks?'

She waved her hand and they appeared around both their necks. 'I think we should wear them so that we can put them on quickly if we need to.'

David nodded. 'Is there anything else on your list?'

'That's everything.' She looked up at him. 'Are you ready?'

'Not yet.'

She watched him walk over to the small cupboard by the bed. He opened it and pulled out an old box. Inside it there was a Swiss Army knife and a compass that he put in his pocket. Then he lifted out an old photo that looked as though it had been folded and unfolded a thousand times. He stared down at the picture and then bent his head over it and murmured something too quiet for her to hear. When he finally stood and turned to face her the photo was gone, hidden somewhere beneath his T-shirt. With a jolt to her heart she realised that something about him had changed. Despite his ordinary clothes he no longer stood in front of her as a boy, but as a soldier prepared for battle.

His voice was firm. 'I'm ready.'

She nodded and looked toward her globe in time to see Amurru emerge. He shuffled over and stopped in front of David. 'On behalf of the High Council of Genesia, I express our sincere gratitude for what you are about to do.'

Before David could answer he turned to Kora and taking her hand sank to one knee. 'Be safe, Empress,' he said and touched her hand to his bowed head. 'I will eagerly await your return.' She thought she saw the sheen of moisture in his eyes as he released her and turned away without another word.

Speechless, she simply glanced at David and then, with a wave of her hand, shimmered them both to one of the most isolated places in Australia — the Simpson Desert.

Yesterday's web

The sun had risen on the desert turning the landscape a magnificent golden red. They had planned to do this at night but now it somehow seemed fitting that they would travel at the dawn of a new day because the outcome, for good or for bad, would also bring the dawn of a new era for Genesia.

David had been quiet since their arrival. 'How much longer do we have to wait?'

'About ten more minutes.'

'You look tired.'

'Thank you,' she said. 'So do you.'

She was glad to see a small smile tug at his mouth. 'I only meant to ask if it will affect your powers.'

'Maybe a little.' She shrugged. 'But it cannot be helped. Even if we waited to do this I think it would be impossible for me to sleep now.'

Emptiness stretched out around them and David

moved to stand in front of her, his face serious. 'I want you to know, Kora, that no matter how this turns out I will have no regrets.'

'Even if Vennum kills you?'

'The chance to see my father again is more than I could have hoped for.' He reached out and gently grasped her hand. 'And I hope that you get the chance to see your father again, too.'

The sincerity in his voice brought the sting of tears to her eyes and she quickly blinked them away. Pulling her hand out of his she turned. 'I think we have waited long enough.'

Kora stood with her back to the sun, the golden rays forming a shimmering halo around her. She lifted her arms and centred her power. The location was easy to find. They were going back to the cave where they had found his father's blood. But the time would be harder. They had to go back five years, to the day his father had been reported missing. The time of day had been an even harder decision to make. They knew from the official Army report that he had last been seen at 3.00 pm. David's watch had stopped at 3.17. In the end they had decided they would return to 2.50 pm and, with a little luck, see David's father in the last moments of his life.

Kora focused, summoning all her power until her

chest ached with the force of it as she pushed her way back through the heavy glue of time. She gasped for air as the weight of the years squeezed her lungs. She felt like she was drowning in time. Finally, there was a flash of light and a tiny pinprick of a portal opened in front of her. She closed her eyes, summoned every last drop of her power and forced it to open further. She groaned with the effort, it was like swimming through mud. Then finally, with an exhausted moan, she dropped to the ground.

'You did it.'

David's excited voice reached her and she struggled to pull herself up. 'Vennum,' was all she could manage to say.

She felt David's strong hands clasp her and pull her to her feet. They only had seconds before Vennum would be after them. Without hesitation David dragged her to the portal and jumped through, pulling her with him.

They landed on the other side with a thud and covered in a sticky layer of something that resembled a spider's web. She immediately turned back to the portal and, with a sigh of relief, closed it down.

'Are you okay?' David was kneeling beside her looking worried. 'Was Vennum there?'

'I am okay, I think.' She sat for a moment resting her head on her knees. 'I did not see Vennum, but he will be there now.' She lifted her head to give him a small smile.

'That was a lot of power. I thought for a moment I was not going to be able to do it.'

'But you did do it, Kora.' David reached out to help her to her feet. 'I think we'd be safer inside the cave. In case someone sees us.'

Kora scanned the barren landscape. 'Only a human would want to go to the middle of a war zone.'

'Come on,' he said. He pulled her towards the cave.

They stepped into the familiar darkness. 'There is no one in here,' she said.

David walked to the wall of the cave. 'There's no blood on the wall.' His voice was hoarse. 'My father — he's still alive!'

A blast from the past

Kora stepped out of the cave into the bright sunlight. Hot wind whirled around her, lifting the dry, powdery sand and whipping her hair into her eyes. She would have shielded herself from the heat, but she needed to save every ounce of magic to open the time-travel portal to return home. She squinted into the afternoon glare.

David stepped out of the cave and stood beside her. Below them the desert sands stretched away for as far as they could see, disappearing into a cloudy haze on the horizon.

'Come on,' said Kora, clambering down the hillside. She was exhausted but knew they did not have much time. 'We have found our hiding place inside the cave, now we need to find somewhere out here to hide before your father comes.'

David nodded. They scrambled about two hundred metres from the cave to a place where five tall boulders jutted up from the ground like the grotesque fingers of some long-dead giant. They squeezed in through one of the wider gaps to stand in the centre. The fingers of rock towered around them like a cage. 'This should give us some cover,' she said, 'no matter which direction your father comes from.'

'How long do you think we have to wait?'

'Not long. A few minutes at the most.'

David dropped his backpack onto the sand and leaned against one of the boulders, his eyes scanning the desert. 'You know, Kora, I still can't believe I'm about to see my father again, after all these years. It seems like we are doing the impossible.'

'I know. Even for a genie, this is an unbelievable thing to be doing.'

David turned to face her. 'I keep wondering, if my father wasn't killed by an enemy soldier, then how was he killed? Was it an accidental death? Did he fall off a cliff? Did a wild animal attack him?'

Kora nodded. 'At least we will not have to wait and wonder for much longer.'

'There's something else I keep wondering about, Kora.' David spoke quickly, his voice strange, wavery. 'What if my father can be saved? What if he is attacked by a wild animal and we can stop it?' She heard the hope creeping into his voice. 'What if he is injured, and bleeding to death, but we can get him to a hospital?' He reached out and grabbed Kora's hands. 'It's possible, isn't it?'

'I do not know, David.' She smiled sadly at him. 'I just do not know.' Kora thought about everything she had learned on the theory of time travel. 'It is not known whether history can be changed during time travel. But most Genesians believe that it cannot.' She watched his face. 'They not only believe that you cannot change history, they believe it would be wrong to do so.'

He nodded, but she could still see the hope in his eyes. He turned to gaze out between the boulders again. 'Where are they?' he murmured. 'It must be almost time.'

She turned to scan the horizon in the other direction. The hot wind whipped the dry desert sand up into squalling dust clouds. Finally a few faint sounds came to them.

David grabbed her arm. 'Did you hear that?'

She nodded. They peered in the direction of the sounds. Then they saw them. A small contingent of soldiers materialising out of the swirling dust. They were mostly on foot, marching in front of a jeep, and were heading out from around the base of a distant rocky outcrop.

'We're miles away, Kora,' said David. The glare from the afternoon sun was blinding and he shielded his eyes with his hand, straining to see. 'And they're not even heading this way.'

She glanced up at the nearby cave where they knew his father was soon to die. 'No wonder they did not ever find your father,' she whispered. 'It is so far from where they would have been looking for him.'

David turned to her, his face anxious. 'We'll never see anything from here, Kora.' He grabbed her hands. 'Can you spare the energy to shimmer us a bit closer?'

She looked at his panicked expression. She couldn't let him down. Not now that they had come this far. She gave one quick nod. 'I have to be able to.'

He slung his backpack over his shoulder and she shimmered them both into a position slightly ahead of where the men were marching. Further out in the desert there were less places to hide, but they managed to find a boulder just big enough for them both to crouch behind.

They huddled down, back to back, peering around the rock. The Australian soldiers were marching almost directly ahead of them now, trudging heavily, guns slung over their shoulders.

'Can you see your father yet, David?'

He shook his head. 'But I know he was rostered on as one of the rear guards the day he died.' He glanced back at her. 'Today, I mean.'

Kora nodded. Some distance behind the jeep, almost completely shrouded in the clouds of dust, she could just make out the ghostly shapes of two or three soldiers. One of those men had to be David's father.

David was tense beside her. 'Stay here,' she whispered. 'Do not do anything stupid.'

The jeep rolled by them, and then the rear guards were there. They could make out the men more clearly now they were closer.

'I see him, Kora,' he said. 'It's him, there, the one closest to us.'

For one wild moment Kora thought David was going to sprint the short distance across the sand to his father. She turned to grab at his shirt, but then everything dissolved into chaos. A flash of light streaked through the air above his father's head, slicing open a hole in the empty sky, and a man wearing a strange, bright red coat fell through it. He dropped out of the sky right on top of David's father, the two of them falling to the ground in a tangled heap. It happened so fast that David's father didn't have time to react.

Kora stared, mouth gaping. She couldn't believe her eyes. She recognised the man in the red coat! 'It is Rihando,' she croaked.

David's father barely had time to yell before another

group of Genesian men materialised out of thin air just metres away from them. Rihando sprang to his feet and grabbed David's father, hauling him up by an arm. He waved his hand in the direction of the men charging towards him and an explosion of sand flew up from the ground in front of them. The flying sand surrounded everyone in a thick blanket that was impossible to see through.

David and Kora stood staring into the swirling cloud. It had all happened in less than ten seconds, and the other Australian soldiers must have seen or heard something unusual because they were returning to investigate. But when the hot wind cleared away the dust cloud everyone, David's father included, had vanished.

Murder on the dark

David grabbed her arm. 'We need to get back to the cave.'

'No, it is too dangerous. I think I saw —'

'I wish,' said David, before she could finish, 'to return to the cave, now!'

Using the tiniest amount of magic possible she shimmered them into their hiding spot inside the cave. She blinked, willing her eyes to adjust to the darkness after the glare of the sun outside.

The previously empty cave was now crowded and noisy. 'Far out,' said David, squinting. 'That's Vennum!'

'That is what I was trying to tell you,' she whispered. 'And his harnessed genies have got Rihando surrounded.'

A younger-looking Vennum stepped out from the darkest shadows of the cave. 'Well, isn't this lovely,' he said to Rihando. 'The Emperor's most trusted and loyal genie will be helping me rule Genesia.'

Some of the genies laughed but many of the others

looked sympathetically at Rihando. 'You are truly mad if you believe you can, or ever will, rule Genesia,' said Rihando, quietly. 'You will never conquer the city walls.'

'It is you who is mad if you thought fleeing to Earth would save you from me.' Vennum sneered. 'And harnessing yourself to a human won't work either.'

All eyes turned to David's father who was leaning against the back wall of the cave, holding his arm with its burning welt from harnessing.

'I did not harness myself to him,' spat Rihando. 'I fell on top of him by accident trying to escape you.'

'It matters not. What is done is easily undone.' He turned to the genie on his right. 'I wish for a dagger.'

'No!' Rihando and David both cried out at the same time as the deadly weapon materialised in the palm of Vennum's hand.

Kora felt David move beside her and she gripped tightly onto his shirt to hold him in place. 'You cannot let him see us. If Vennum finds us here together now he will recognise that I am from the future.' She whispered the words hurriedly at David to hold him still. 'That means he will be able to find us, and the rest of your family, when he comes looking for me in the future.'

'Then you stay here.' David shook free of Kora. 'He doesn't know who I am.'

Rihando had moved to stand between Vennum and David's father. 'It is not the human's fault,' he said. 'If he simply wishes me unharnessed you can spare him.'

Vennum shrugged, but as Rihando turned he came face-to-face with David's father's machine gun. 'Back out of the cave,' he said. 'All of you.'

Vennum laughed and David's father stepped closer, his gun held steady, finger on the trigger. 'Back out, I said.'

'Your weapon will not harm us,' said Rihando.

Vennum spun the dagger in his hand. 'I had forgotten how entertaining Earth can be.'

Rihando ignored him. 'You must understand,' he implored David's father. 'I am a genie and when I fell on you it accidentally harnessed me to you. Unless you wish to set me free he will kill you.'

In that moment everything changed. David's father opened fire on the genies but all the bullets fell uselessly to the ground. The noise in the cave was deafening. Vennum ordered his genies to control Rihando and an enormous genie fight broke out leaving David's father completely unprotected. And then Vennum threw the dagger. It hurtled through the air and lodged deep into his father's chest. Blood oozed everywhere and David's father slumped back against the cave wall.

'No, David,' croaked Kora, as David flew out from

their hiding spot and ran to his father.

David pushed his way through the genies to reach his father. 'Dad,' groaned David, helping his father to the ground.

'David?' asked his father. 'Is that really you?'

'Yes, Dad. Don't ask how, but it's really me.'

'I must be dreaming,' said his father. 'Because my only wish was to see you again before I die.' He lifted his hand from his wound and stared at the blood that dripped from his fingers.

'You're not going to die,' said David, fiercely. 'I won't let you.' David looked up frantically at Rihando, who was heavily surrounded by genies, and then looked in Kora's direction. 'Do something,' he shouted.

Grief tore at her heart. What was she supposed to do? She could not heal his father and even if Rihando shimmered them to a hospital, not only did she doubt that the doctors could save him but Vennum would only follow them and kill him the second they arrived anyway.

David's father gasped for air and David pressed firmly where the dagger was buried in his chest in an attempt to stop the flow of blood.

'It's okay, son,' he said. His father reached up and placed his hand on top of David's. 'I'm so proud of you, David. Take my watch so that you will always remember our time together.' He then lifted both of their blood-covered hands away from the wound and with a loud groan wrenched out the dagger. Blood spurted. His father closed his eyes. 'I love you, son,' he whispered.

Tears streamed down David's face. 'I love you too, Dad.' But it was too late. His father was gone.

David swiped at his tears and when he lifted his head his face was a mask of agony. He picked up the bloodied dagger and slowly stood. Revenge burned blue fire in his eyes as he faced Vennum.

'Good luck, kid,' said Vennum. 'Your father was no match for me, and neither will you be.'

Kora panicked. David would surely die if he attacked Vennum now. They had to get back to their own time. At least there they had a plan.

She slipped out of her hiding spot and at that moment Rihando turned his head in her direction. She saw understanding dawn on his face. Rihando rubbed his wrists where the golden bands had only just faded away and then threw himself at Vennum.

The surprise and agony of harnessing knocked Vennum to the ground and Kora used the opportunity to shimmer them out to the top of the rocky hillside above the cave.

'What are you doing?' shouted David.

'Saving your life. You will not win fighting Vennum here. Our only chance is if we follow our plan.'

David's eyes searched the hillside. 'Will he follow us?'

'Maybe. The harnessing will only buy us a couple of minutes.'

'Rihando gave himself up to Vennum.'

'He did it to save you,' said Kora. 'To save both of us. He saw me in there.'

'It must have been Rihando that sent me my father's watch.' David rubbed his face. 'I knew it hadn't been there all along.'

'Rihando would have felt terrible about your father and would have known his wish for you to have it.'

'Before we go back there's something I have to know, Kora.' He looked her directly in the eyes. 'Did you know Vennum killed my father before we came here today?'

'Of course not.' Her eyes narrowed. 'But I bet that stinking armourowl did.'

'How could he have known?'

Kora shrugged. 'Nobody fully understands the armourowls' ways.'

'Don't be mad at him. I'm glad Amurru chose to make me a part of this.'

'Do you not see how much Amurru has kept hidden from us?' Anger shook her voice. 'How he has manipulated us into his own greater plan?'

'I'm glad I know the truth.'

'Even if it ends up killing you?'

'Vennum has to answer for what he has done. If only he had given my father time to understand what was going on, he could have freed Rihando. Then my father would still be alive today.'

Her eyes scanned the hillside looking for any sign they had been followed. 'You know Amurru was insistent that we have a plan for our return. I guess that means he knew we would not be able to change the past.'

David shook his head from side to side, examining the bloodied dagger in his hands. 'I wasn't able to change the past.' But then he lifted his head and his face had such a look of brutal determination that it sent a cold shiver hurtling down her spine. 'But I swear to you, I will change the future.'

The battle begins

Kora and David found a sheltered spot on the hillside above the cave. She was fairly sure that all the genies had returned to Genesia now. They must have decided that one human boy wasn't worth chasing after. But, just in case, she wanted to be out of sight when she began to summon her magic. She didn't need to be fighting Vennum on this side of the time-travel portal as well as on the other.

Kora sucked in a deep breath. She was still weak from opening the first portal. Her stomach twisted with nerves. She wasn't sure she had the energy left to open one big enough for them to return. She closed her eyes, needing a few more moments to gather her strength and steady her nerves. 'Let us just run over things one more time.'

David's eyes narrowed impatiently but he simply nodded. 'You're going to open the portal in a different place from where we left.'

'Yes,' she agreed. 'Higher up the side of the rocky slope. I will try to open it so that we step through behind that boulder you said looked like a dragon's head. That way we will be able to see how many of them there are before they spot us.'

David looked at the dagger in his hand, still covered in his father's blood, and his brow furrowed. 'And it will give us time to prepare ourselves and to set off the chloroform bomb.'

'Yes, but it will not be much time, David. They will be waiting for us and on the alert for any use of magic at all. They will feel the magic before we have even climbed through the portal. We may only have a few seconds to get ready, David. If we are lucky.'

He nodded. 'It'll be enough. Stop worrying, Kora. Vennum's army are all genies.' David's mouth twisted in a grim smile. 'We both know they can't harm me. I'm human.'

'David!' She stared at him, aghast. 'You do not know what you are saying.'

He shrugged. 'Look, Kora, whatever happens, happens. Let's just do it.' He twirled the dagger in his hand and then tucked it into his belt. 'I'm as ready as I'll ever be.'

Kora nodded and let her magic rumble around in her

chest, testing. It was definitely weaker. She stood taller, letting it fill her.

David lifted his gasmask to cover his face and pulled the chloroform bomb out of his backpack, ready to use. He moved to stand close beside her.

Lifting her own gasmask to cover her face she turned and focused her thoughts on a clear space just above ground level about a metre in front of them, and released a solid stream of power. She was ready this time for the heavy resistance she felt as she channelled her power. Instead of the instant flash of light that signalled the opening of a portal, there was a slow quivering in the air as she forced the portal through space and time. It seemed to take much longer to open than the first portal, and she began to wonder if she had the strength left to force it forward far enough in time. But finally the quivering light in the air in front of them steadied, splitting and opening into a small hole about the size of a shoebox. Breathing heavily, she drew in more and more power, until her body shook with the effort. She dropped to her knees, struggling to breathe, struggling to hold the portal open.

Power surged in her chest. Her fingers and toes began to tingle. Still she needed more. Before them the portal flashed and shuddered, stretching wider bit by tiny bit. She had to be quick. With a final gasp, she flung every last ounce of energy into the flow of magic pouring from her chest. It drained from her, surging into the tiny window in time she was opening before them. It felt as though her own life force was draining away along with it.

Her vision blurred and she blinked rapidly. She had to stay focused and hold the portal open long enough for them both to squeeze through. The portal shuddered and faltered several times before finally steadying itself. It was still small. Not even up to her waist. Still, she was sure they could both crawl through it, one at a time.

'Hurry, David,' she gasped.

David stared at the tiny portal. As soon as he could see a small square of the familiar red earth on the other side, he dropped to his knees and wriggled through. Turning, he reached back through the portal and grabbed Kora's hand, hauling her limp body through behind him.

Kora could not hold the portal open another second. She let it slam closed behind her, barely missing her feet. She tried to see what was happening, but she was having trouble turning her head. Sticky strands of web clung to her gasmask, obscuring her vision. She was too weak to even lift her hand to swipe at them. The dome of blue sky above her wavered and spun and a crushing weight pressed down on her chest. She wondered vaguely if her lungs were collapsing.

She tried to focus on David. She knew they had only seconds before they would be attacked. She had to know what was going on. She managed to turn her head just far enough to see David peering around the side of the dragon's head rock. At least she had managed to open the portal in the right place!

She tried to speak, to ask him what he could see, but she couldn't move her lips. But then David spun around and sprang towards her, his face white behind his mask. He positioned himself in front of her and pulled out the lever on the chloroform gas bottle. 'They're coming, Kora.' She could barely hear him over the ringing in her ears and the hissing of the chloroform. 'And there's hundreds of them.'

Trick or trap?

It took less than a second for the rocky slope in front of them to be overrun by genies, many of whom Kora recognised. There were men and women, old and young, but by far the majority of them were young men. Genesia's finest fighting men, stolen for Vennum's evil army!

Terrified and unable to move, Kora wondered if David was about to die and she was about to be harnessed. But it was amazing. The chloroform was streaming from the gas bottle and, unbelievably, their plan was actually working. The chloroform was so effective, the genies were barely able to materialise before they dropped to the ground, unconscious. They didn't even have time to warn the others before they were knocked out.

Kora knew it wouldn't keep them out of action for long, but hopefully it would be long enough to get at Vennum. David's head was frantically turning every which way, scanning each genie that appeared in an effort to spot Vennum. Where was he?

'It's him!' cried David, dropping the hissing gas bottle and leaping away from her. David's voice cut through the roaring in her ears and she turned her head to look in the direction he was running. Just metres in front of them Vennum had materialised. With his jet black hair and dark, crazed eyes, and his body covered in harnessing scars, she would recognise him anywhere.

She watched as he finished shimmering into view. He had barely materialised when his dark eyes met hers and, in the tiny moment before he fell to his knees, she saw the light of recognition dawn in them.

David had drawn his dagger and with a cry of rage flew towards Vennum as Vennum's body sagged to the ground, unconscious.

Kora tried to push herself up to see what was happening, but the extra effort made her dizzy. She watched as David raised the dagger over Vennum's prone body, but then he hesitated. Kora strained higher to see what was wrong. Black dots swam before her eyes. Was she seeing things? Vennum's unconscious body began to shimmer and blur around the edges. His body shrank, and the long strands of greasy hair shimmered into a wild mop of shiny black curls. Vennum had transformed into her brother, Atym!

She tried to call out to David to stop but her lips refused to move. The whole world was spinning as she gasped for air. Her vision contracted until all she could see was David's shocked gaze as he turned his head to look at her, the knife still suspended in the air above her brother's heart. Then her strength gave out and she slumped into the red dust.

She forced her lungs to expand and pulled in a couple of long breaths. If only she could get rid of the gasmask. Slowly her vision cleared enough to be able to make out some of what was happening around her.

She tilted her head to the side, trying to spot David. How close he had come to killing her brother! She shuddered at the thought. Vennum must have wished for Atym to transform into a likeness of himself.

Her eyes roamed over the mounds of unconscious genies, searching for the real Vennum. A couple of them were already beginning to stir. There wasn't much time before the chloroform would wear off. When that happened, and all the genies woke up, Kora knew they wouldn't have a chance. Then her eyes fell on Rihando's familiar red coat. There was something odd about the way he was slumped on the ground. His back and head were propped up against a rock, almost as if he were simply sitting there with his eyes closed. She hoped he was okay.

Struggling to summon some magic, Kora attempted to heal herself. She had to get herself together to help David. But there was nothing left, and the effort just left her gasping again.

Then a voice she knew echoed down the desert slope.

'So we meet again, soldier's son.'

Her eyes flew to the sound. About half way up the hill, upwind of the chloroform gas, stood Vennum, a heavy machine gun pointed straight at David's chest.

David was still crouched next to Atym, his face a mask of horror at what he had almost done. Now he slowly pushed himself to his feet and turned to face Vennum, the dagger still clutched in one hand.

Vennum laughed, his crazy, wild voice echoing loudly around the barren hillside. 'You haven't changed a bit in the five years since I last saw you, boy,' he screeched. 'I should have guessed that you would be the human Kora would choose for harnessing.' He laughed again and Kora could see the madness in his whirling eyes.

'That was a cowardly thing to do, Vennum,' called David, nodding at Atym's small, limp body. 'Sacrificing a child to save yourself.'

Vennum laughed again, his demented eyes swivelling towards Kora. 'Well, well, well,' he cackled. 'Look at the most powerful genie in the universe now.' She felt his black eyes burning into hers. 'Pathetic! Bah! Can't even raise enough magic to stop a few bullets. I hope you haven't damaged her permanently, soldier's son.'

David pointed the dagger towards Vennum. 'You won't live to find out.'

'Foolish boy,' spat Vennum. 'But it matters not, because in less than a heartbeat, you will be dead.' He cackled. 'And she will be mine, along with all of Genesia.'

She watched in stunned horror as Vennum raised the machine gun higher. Kora had no doubt that it was fully loaded.

David stood tall, and his hand lifted as if to throw the dagger, but Vennum was much too far up the hill for there to be any hope of it reaching him. She had to save David! There was no way he could survive a volley of machine gun fire and she couldn't just watch him die. Kora struggled desperately to gather some power. Even a tiny trickle would be enough to give David a bullet shield. She sucked in a deep breath and tried to pull together some energy, but there was absolutely nothing left. Her body was an empty shell. And she was out of time. The world erupted in an explosion of noise as Vennum let fire with the machine gun. As if in slow motion a spray of bullets burst from the barrel and hurtled toward David.

She concentrated, trying desperately with every last

ounce of her life force to summon forth some magic. But the effort was too much. She collapsed back against the dry earth. They had been defeated. Despair and sorrow overwhelmed her. Almost everyone she cared about was either harnessed or dead. She lay there, wishing the bullets were aimed at her instead, and waited the interminable few seconds she knew it would take before she heard the sound of David's dead body slump to the ground.

Mask of invisibility

Kora closed her eyes and gave herself up to the agony that consumed her. She had failed. A memory of David from when she had first seen him played in front of her eyes. He had seemed so tall and strong. She remembered his curious ocean-blue eyes and how strange and unsettling they had been to her. It was too late now for her to admit that she found them interesting, beautiful even. It was too late now for anything.

An unexpected hammering exploded in the air around her. Bewildered, her eyes flew open and she blinked rapidly, convinced that she must be seeing things. David was surrounded by a thick shield of armour and all of Vennum's bullets were dropping uselessly to the ground. David looked as surprised as she felt.

A flicker of red caught the corner of her eye and she turned her head to meet Rihando's steady gaze. He gave her a wink and a gasmask appeared on his face. He must have seen theirs when they time-travelled back to the cave and known to wear an invisible mask. With a pointed look at the gas bottle Rihando purposefully lifted his hand and removed the mask, then slumped unconscious.

Vennum let out an angry curse. He flung away his now useless weapon and advanced towards David.

The glint of the dagger in David's hand flashed dangerously in the sunlight. She watched in fascination as David lifted his arm and hurled the deadly weapon directly at Vennum.

Vennum dodged to the left, but not quickly enough, and the flying dagger whistled past his head, slicing off a thick chunk of his ear on its way past. Blood spurted violently onto the sand. Vennum's roars of pain echoed in the morning silence while he clutched his head and blood gushed down his neck.

For a moment David just stood there watching, as if in shock, then he bolted for the dagger. Vennum lurched for David before he could reach it and knocked him to the ground. Vennum's eyes were black with pain and rage. She watched, horrified, as Vennum centred all his fury on David like a hurricane singling out a lone palm tree for destruction.

They struggled together on the sand. David was strong but Vennum was completely insane. He had both hands around David's throat. David shoved and kicked, frantically trying to shake the madman off him.

She knew she had to help him. The gas had run out and some of the genies were beginning to stir. Searching her body, she found the tiniest trickle of magic weaving itself back through her. She knew if she used that drop of magic now to help David, she may never get another chance to heal herself.

David shook Vennum off, but Vennum only charged at him again. Kora made her decision. It took all her effort to gather and command that tiny trickle of magic. Breathing heavily and sweating fiercely she conjured a gas grenade in David's hand.

Barely able to hold her eyes open she saw the look of shock on David's face as he stared down at the grenade in his hand. She wanted to shout out to him that it was okay, that it wasn't a real grenade, but her exhausted body refused to cooperate.

David's eyes glinted with a steely determination. Without hesitation he pulled the pin on the grenade and tossed it to the ground. With a soft hiss, the chloroform snaked into the dry desert air.

Darkness reached for her. She saw Vennum's body slump heavily onto David's, but the more she tried to focus on them the more the black dots swirling in front of her eyes got in the way. Unable to fight any longer, Kora finally let the darkness take her.

The price

Kora wanted to open her eyes but her eyelids refused to lift.

'Kora?' The murmuring of voices talking near her finally penetrated her fuzzy head.

She struggled once more with her eyelids and this time managed to prise them apart. Her father's anxious face loomed over her against the backdrop of a clear blue desert sky. 'Am I dead?' she asked.

'No, Empress,' Amurru rasped. 'You live!'

Her father's worried face was directly in front of hers.

'You must rest,' said her father. 'Your body is trying to recover.'

Panic fluttered in her chest as she realised she could not feel any magic within her. She tried to sit up and a golden cushion appeared behind her head.

'Here,' said her father, holding a juice to her lips. 'This will help.'

It was the most delectable nectar she had ever tasted and slowly the fuzziness cleared from her brain and memories came flooding back.

'David?'

'I'm over here.' She turned her head to his voice and met his gorgeous, ocean-blue eyes. 'Trying not to harness any more genies.'

She slumped back against the cushion that was a lot more comfortable than the hard desert ground. Her body may be slow but her head was catching up fast. Of course, David would need to keep away from her father.

'And Vennum?' she asked.

'Unconscious,' said Amurru. 'Thanks to you, Empress.'

'Rihando has taken him to the Slaytians,' said her father. 'They have agreed to unharness all his genies.'

'And then will Rihando banish him from Genesia?'

Her father nodded. 'Vennum will never again be able to return to Genesia and the High Council will begin the difficult task of identifying and sentencing the rogue genies.'

'I am sorry, father.' She placed her hand in her father's and he squeezed it gently. 'I know you did not want to have to bargain with the Slaytians.'

'They are deciding on their price now, but whatever it

is, it will be worth it. I wish for nothing more than to have my family safe and Genesia free once again.'

'And Atym?' She glanced at David as she remembered what had almost happened to her brother. 'He is okay?'

'The little one has learned much,' said Amurru, blinking his yellow eyes. 'And he is a survivor, like his sister.'

She felt the absence of her power. 'I have survived,' she said. 'But I am not the same.'

'Give it time, Kora,' said her father. 'No genie in history has ever wielded that amount of magic. How else do you think I knew to come here?' He smiled at her. 'The ripples were felt even in the Genesian wilderness.'

'And what were you really doing out there?'

She watched her father and Amurru exchange a guarded look. 'It is a story for another time.' Her father reached into his pocket and withdrew her globe, placing it on the cushion next to her. 'Right now all I care about is that you and Atym are safe.'

She took a long, deep drink of her juice and her eyes returned to David. He was covered in blood and dirt. 'What happened?' she asked. 'The last thing I remember is sending you the gas grenade.'

'Crikey,' he said. 'I thought you intended to blow us all up.'

She couldn't help but smile. 'It did not stop you from pulling the pin.'

David shrugged. 'As long as it got rid of Vennum I was all for it.'

'Thank goodness the grenade worked.'

'Like a charm.' David paced as close as he dared to Kora and her father. 'Vennum was out cold in seconds. I put the gasmask back on Rihando and as soon as he woke up he made me a chloroform mask for Vennum.'

'How long will the chloroform mask last?'

David smirked. 'It won't run out like the gas. I had Rihando make it so that the chloroform has a constant supply and then I tied it over Vennum's face. He won't wake up until Rihando and the Slaytians want him to.'

Her father stood and faced David gravely. 'As a father I am deeply grateful to you, David, for all you have done. You have proven yourself to be a human of extreme courage and bravery. As Emperor, on behalf of all of Genesia, I thank you. If there is ever any way we can repay this debt to you then you need only ask.'

'Thank you, sir,' said David. 'But my wish has already been granted.'

'Not quite,' said Kora. 'We still need to find your father's body and bring it home.'

'I will investigate this myself.' The Emperor bowed his

head. 'You have my word.'

Kora managed to shove her foot into Amurru who was waiting silently beside her. 'Do not think we do not know what part you played in all of this,' she accused. 'You and your sneaky creation magic, making sure that of all the people and places on Earth, that I should end up harnessed to the son of a human that Vennum had killed!'

'I beg your forgiveness, Empress,' said Amurru, not looking the least bit sorry and shuffling away out of kicking distance. 'I only allowed it to be, the rest you created for yourselves.'

Kora wanted to be angry with Amurru, but it was at that moment that she felt it — the tiniest trickle of her power returning.

Her father must have realised for his face relaxed into a genuine smile. 'You are healing!'

'Yes,' she said, relieved. She was feeling stronger by the second now.

'No magic for a little while. Let your body fully heal first.' Her father looked at David. 'And no wishes.'

Amurru's yellow eyes blinked slowly. 'You are summoned, Emperor,' he said. 'The Slaytians are decided.'

Her father brushed her long, dark hair back from her face. 'I must go,' he said. 'Stay here and rest a little longer. I will return to you shortly.'

'Tell Atym that I miss him.' She smiled. 'Just a little bit.'

Her father leaned down and kissed her forehead. Then he stepped back and glanced around at the barren desert and the hot sun glaring down on them. He waved his hand and Kora slowly drifted up through the air to land on a comfortable bed. A shady canopy appeared above them, and a table laden with food and drinks appeared beside them.

'I am so proud of you, my daughter,' he said. And then he slowly shimmered away.

Amurru placed a stumpy hand on hers. 'I, too, am glad you are safe, Empress.' His eyes flickered to David. 'And you, too, my human friend.' With an ache in her chest she realised how old and tired Amurru looked now. 'I must go and check in with the High Council.'

'My mother?' she asked.

'I will make sure she has been informed.' Amurru bowed his head and shuffled away. 'Do not worry, Empress.'

David flopped onto the ground next to her, his eyes still filled with concern. 'Are you really all right?' he asked.

'I think so.' She hoped so. She could feel her strength very slowly returning.

'When I saw you unconscious, I thought,' he raked a

hand over his head, 'I thought you were dead.'

'I thought I was dying.' She looked him over, taking in his blood-stained clothes and skin. 'How about you, are you okay?'

'Yeah, nothing a hot shower won't fix.'

She smiled. 'Sorry I cannot help you with that right now.'

He rubbed a hand across the scar on his arm. 'Guess I'll have to get used to that.'

She frowned. Did he think she would not get her power back? 'What do you mean by that?'

'When your father returns for us, I will wish you unharnessed.' David took a deep breath and his eyes looked kind of sad. 'You deserve to go home, Kora. You deserve to be with your family.'

She looked at this amazing human boy in front of her. 'You would really do that?'

He nodded. 'And I can't believe I'm going to say this, but I think I will actually even miss you.'

She grinned. 'You will not need to miss me too soon. I cannot return home until the High Council of Genesia deems my duty served. If they force me to stay here on Earth, then — and I cannot believe I am going to say this — I would rather be harnessed to you than to anybody else.'

'You really think they will make you stay?'

She shrugged. 'I actually want to stay on for a bit.' She gave him a playful nudge. 'You have not even shown me any pandas yet.'

David smiled and this time it reached all the way up to crinkle the corners of his ocean-blue eyes. 'You know you really aren't what I expected in a genie.'

She smiled back at him, her eyes dancing. 'Well, you are not exactly what I expected in a human, either.'

David picked up her hand and then looked shyly down to where his fingers encircled hers. 'Guess that means we're stuck with each other, then.'

She looked at their entwined hands. How different she felt now to the genie that had arrived here on Earth just weeks ago. Everything had changed. She had changed. She lifted her eyes to his and noticed he was blushing. 'Yes,' she said, smiling up at him. 'I guess we are.'

The End

Acknowledgements

We would like to thank Cate Sutherland and the fabulous team at Fremantle Press. Thank you, Cate, for your endless support and advice.

To our wonderful husbands, Lindsay and Mark, thank you both for your infinite love and support, and for your long-suffering patience in never being able to use the telephone line. To Dan, thank you for your expert advice. To our beautiful family, Beryl, Ken, Marion, Brian, Ron, Jo, Kellie, Russell, Kate, Sarah, Naomi and Rachael, thank you all for your unwavering love and encouragement. And thank you to our other amazing family and friends who have supported us along the way, you know who you are. We love you all.

The authors

Jennifer McBride and Lynda Nixon were born and raised in Western Australia. They each have a husband, two daughters and a troublesome cat. They are sisters who have shared a lifelong love of reading and writing and have enjoyed writing their first novel together.

First published 2013 by
FREMANTLE PRESS
25 Quarry Street, Fremantle 6160
Western Australia
www.fremantlepress.com.au

Cover design by Tracey Gibbs.
Printed by 1010, China.

National Library of Australia
Cataloguing-in-publication data

McBride, Jennifer and Lynda Nixon
Shimmer

Edition: 1st ed.

ISBN: 978 1 922089 43 4 (pbk.)

A823

Fremantle Press is supported by the State Government
through the Department of Culture and the Arts.

Government of **Western Australia**
Department of **Culture and the Arts**

Publication of this title was assisted by the Commonwealth Government through
the Australia Council, its arts funding and advisory body.